SWITCH

And

Blue Eagle

A Superhero Sidekick Novel

Joseph "TienSwitch" Safdia

Book Cover by FujiFingerZ.

First Edition: March 2025

Chapter 1

Jack watched outside his bedroom window as Mareplane streaked by in the distance. At first, he thought it was a common commercial jet flying over the clouds, but a closer look allowed him to notice the four galloping legs of the radiant metal horse with airplane wings.

He sighed and focused back on the article he was reading on his laptop. And then he focused on the feeling of peace and quiet, rare commodities in his life.

It was a lazy Saturday afternoon, and Jack Dufraine was happy to have it. He looked around his room, gazing at his metal band and pro-wrestling posters as he took in this moment of tranquility. His father was working at the insurance office and he was done with his homework, which meant he had the house to himself. It was a chance to focus on the article he was reading, "A New Way To Fight Crime: Social Justice, Rehabilitation, and Crime Prevention", without interruption.

And that's when he felt and heard the buzzing. He pulled his phone out of his black cargo pants and saw that a notification appeared. It was the police scanner app. His heart sank when he read the alert.

Jack shot to his feet. He ran a hand through his black hair, brushing a lock of it away from his eyebrow. His father would get annoyed if he didn't get it cut soon, or started styling it again so it was neater and more clean cut.

But that didn't matter right now. It was time for action.

He scrolled through his contacts and initiated the call.

"Dad, we have a situation," he said.

The insurance brokerage was only twenty minutes away by air. It was quiet on Saturdays. The brokers usually came in when it was time to close a deal with a client not available during the week.

David Dufraine was one of those brokers right now.

When the client came in, he first admired the myriad of pictures and accolades around David's office. Not the sales awards, but the newspaper clippings.

Clippings with titles like "Blue Eagle Saves City Yet Again!" and "Blue Eagle Brings the Villain Gravitational Paul to Justice".

One paper had a photo of David in his blue tights, the eagle logo prominently displayed on his chest. He had a proud smile on his face as his arm was around the shoulder of his then-12 year old son, Jack.

"Herald City's New Father-Son Duo: Blue Eagle Announces Son 'Switch the Blue Eaglet' as Sidekick".

The photos from his younger years showed him with a full head of short black hair. Now, in his early fifties, his hair was graying and receding. But he still looked as fit as any man his age could wish to be. His arms, legs, and chest were massive, and he *looked* like he could punch through a brick wall.

Looks could be deceiving. But, in this case, they weren't.

Now he and the client were talking insurance. Property and casualty insurance. David was just finishing telling the client why property insurance was so important in establishing and protecting what's yours when his phone rang.

"Excuse me one moment," he said politely, picking up the phone. "Hi, Jack."

"Dad, we have a situation," came the voice of his son.

David's brow furrowed. "What is it this time?"

"There's a robbery in progress at Herald City BioGenetics Research Lab. The goons doing it are working for Blizz Kid."

"I'm on my way," assured David, disconnecting the call. He put on an apologetic smile. "I apologize for this, but duty calls."

"I understand," assured the client with a chuckle. "Go get 'em."

"Thank you. Someone else will be here in a few minutes to reschedule our appointment," said David as he raced out of the office.

Moments later on the roof, David discarded his suit and tie, revealing a blue spandex costume with white gloves, boots, belt, and a cape. A white eagle insignia was proudly visible on his massive chest.

Blue Eagle took to the skies.

Meanwhile, Jack had just removed his black T-shirt, cargo pants, and socks and tossed them aside.

Now wearing the same costume as his father, Switch the Blue Eaglet was ready for action.

Chapter 2

Jasper Clemens watched as an armed man waved a gun in the face of a spectacled scientist, barking commands to stand with the others. The scientist obeyed, rushing over to join the rest of the terrified research team of Herald City BioGenetics Research Lab.

There were eight gunmen in the spacious lab. Two long tables stretching the rectangular room held all sorts of equipment. Beakers, Bunsen burners, measuring devices, gas tanks, everything a lab could need. The sunlight from the large window along one side of the room made the overhead lights unnecessary.

It also made their daytime attack that much more brazen.

Jasper grasped his pistol, feeling the knot in his stomach tighten. He glanced toward the double metal doors at the end of the lab, opposite of the wooden doors they had forced a security guard to open for them before knocking him out. The rest of the group was in there getting the thing they came for, and he wished they'd come out already before something bad happened.

"Stop moving!"

His attention shifted over to one of the over a dozen scientists standing against the wall. The researcher's nervous, twitchy movements were angering one of the gunmen.

"I said stop moving!" demanded the thug again, holding his assault rifle to the terrified man's temple.

Jasper approached them and slowly pushed the muzzle of the gun away from the whimpering scientist. The other thug backed away as Jasper turned to the scientist.

"Hey, friend, calm down. Breathe," said Jasper in as soothing a voice as he could manage. The faint hint of an Irish accent could be heard. "We ain't here to hurt you. We ain't here for you guys at all. We're just here to steal your latest project. Hang on tight and this will all be over soon. You got me?"

The scientist gave a frightened nod. He took a ragged but deep breath as he tried to center himself.

Another gunman scoffed. "You always did have a soft spot for these people," he said with a sadistic glint in his eye. "I like to scare these eggheads until they're stone cold white."

Jasper glanced at the man. He was perhaps the most dangerous of their group, and acted as the de facto leader. While the rest of them wore beige jackets lined with wool on the inside, he wore a white tank top that showed off an array of tattoos. Jasper didn't know what the symbols tattooed on his shaved head meant, but they were probably bad.

Jasper stepped toward the man. "Come on, Clay. This is just a job," he whispered, leaning towards him. "No need to make things any worse for them than we have to."

Clay let out a short, defiant laugh. "Clemens, you'll never get it. A job? Do what you love and you'll never have to work a day in your life. Well, I'll tell you I ain't working." He nodded to the other gunman. "If

Shaky over there moves again, shoot off one of his limbs."

The scientist whimpered. The gunman glanced back and forth between them before nodding.

Jasper pressed his lips and turned away. He wasn't about to say anything else. Clay was a dangerous man even by the standards of people that Jasper usually worked with. He didn't want to get on Clay's bad side. Many a man and woman have made the mistake of doing so, and it was the last mistake they ever made.

He jumped a bit when Clay's hand grasped his shoulder. "What's wrong, Jasper? You gotta relax and enjoy the good things in life," he said with a threatening smile on his face. "This is the best part of the job. We're literally God to these people right now."

Jasper felt sick hearing that. "I getcha, Clay. But that's not why I'm here, you know? I'm just in it for the cash." Not wanting to sound like he was challenging Clay, he gave as sincere a smile as he could and added, "I become rich, I can do whatever I want, right? Talk about having power over others."

Clay scoffed. "A pushover like you ain't becoming that rich." He wrapped his arm around Jasper and held him uncomfortably close, using his free hand to point his machine gun at the terrified scientists. "Look, a job like this is the right kind to earn your keep and then some. But in a city full of masks and capes, regular folk like us need to remind everyone that we are just as much a force to be feared as any supervillain."

He pointed his rifle toward the metal doors. A sign that said "Caution: Sensitive Experiments in Progress" was displayed prominently next to it.

"You need to enjoy this feeling. You know why?" he continued. Jasper shook his head. "Because any moment now, the boss is gonna bust through that door with the goods and we're gonna all go back to the hideout and get our money, and this will all be over."

A door burst open. But it wasn't the one they were looking at.

Splintered wood scattered across the room, startling everyone inside as the Father-Son Duo confidently strode in. Both wore identical blue costumes with white capes and eagle insignias on their chests. Blue Eagle, even in his early fifties, looked to be the pinnacle of strength. The lean Switch looked far skinnier than he actually was standing next to his father.

Clay gave a half-hearted shrug. "Or that could happen."

Jasper's blood ran cold.

Blue Eagle looked around the room. "You all must be new to Herald City if you thought it was a good idea to commit such a brazen robbery on a Saturday afternoon, so let me introduce myself. I am Blue Eagle and this is my sidekick, Switch the Blue Eaglet," he announced. "We are among the top superheroes in a city known to be the superhero capital of the world, and you are a group of disposable villain henchmen holding hostages."

"We recommend putting your guns down and backing away from the hostages," advised Switch. "Otherwise, this is a fight that will go really badly for you."

Glancing at his fellow henchmen, Jasper felt his whole world sink. He couldn't get arrested for this. He needed to complete this job. And yet, there was nothing they could do against *superheroes*.

He began to lower his gun toward the ground.

"Ha! I ain't about to be threatened by a 14 year old in tights!" shouted Clay with a smile on his face as if he were having a great time. He opened fire on Switch.

"15, actually," muttered Switch, standing tall as the bullets bounced off of him. He sighed. "They always choose this option."

Jasper watched in horror as the others also opened fire on the heroes. This was only going to make things worse for them!

He dove behind a table. Maybe he could get out without them noticing. Or maybe he could hide out the entire fight without anyone realizing he was there. Either way, he was not about to take on one of Herald City's most famous superhero duos with nothing but a pistol.

Not wanting to get hit by gunfire, Blue Eagle took a low profile and pushed off his feet towards two gunmen. They didn't even have time to react as he shoulder tackled one and punched the other across the jaw, knocking them both out.

Another gunman fired his gun in a panic as Switch rushed him. Bullets pinging off the teen's chest as Switch tackled him to the ground and slammed his fist into the man's forearm to loosen his grip on the rifle. He grabbed the weapon and swung it at his forehead, breaking the gun and knocking the criminal out.

A faint sound slightly touched Blue Eagle's ears. A sound so soft, only *he* could hear it.

The sound of a sharp breath being drawn. The sort of breath one makes when taking aim with a gun.

He whirled around and faced the henchman pointing a gun at him. His eyes glowed red as beams of light fired from them, knocking the gun out of the man's hand.

One henchman reared his arm back and threw a punch at the back of Switch's head. The boy didn't so much as move. The thug, however, screamed in pain and hunched over as he clutched his injured hand.

"It's called invulnerability, doofus. When I have it activated, *nothing* can hurt me. Not even a supernova," boasted Switch. He scoffed. "You literally saw *bullets* bouncing off of me. What did you think a punch in the head was gonna do?"

"Hey, kid, is her head as bulletproof as yours?"

Switch turned to see that Clay had grabbed one of the scientists. He held her close to him, his arm pressed against her chest, as he pulled a revolver out of his back pocket and pressed the muzzle against her head.

"I think her head would explode like a melon at this range," taunted the criminal. He moved his hand and pressed it against the back of her neck, almost as if he was placing something on her. "This magnum is modified. High caliber rounds. It doesn't put a hole in its target. It disintegrates it.

"Let her go," demanded Switch through gritted teeth.

A smirk came across Clay's face as he pushed the scientist's head down and turned the gun on Switch. "I think you'd make a better target."

That was Switch's chance. He rushed forward. "I said let her go!"

Suddenly, there was a wall of ice between them. A wall of actual ice that just formed out of nowhere, six feet tall and a foot thick.

Switch came to a quick stop before getting caught in the ice. He turned toward the source of the strange phenomena.

"Blizz Kid!" he shouted.

The metal doors to the next lab were open. From the room emerged a boy about Switch's age. He wore a heavy blue coat that had fur lining the inside. His hood was up and a pair of ski goggles covered his eyes, though they didn't quite cover up his light blue irises. And they did absolutely nothing to hide his pale white skin.

"Switch. Good to see you," said the supervillain, Blizz Kid.

"Liar," said Switch.

"Yep, I'm lying. Like, here's another lie for you. I won't hurt these scientists."

Blizz Kid turned toward the scientists and fired a blue beam at them from the palm of his gloved hands. They let out a brief cry as they were engulfed. In less than two seconds, all but the woman Clay had attacked were frozen in one large block of ice.

"Now, Switch, if I were you, I'd listen to this next part. It's important," he said as two henchmen appeared out of the room behind him. One carried a large box over his shoulder. "I have some chilling news for you."

"Did you really just use the word 'chilling'?" groaned Switch.

"Fun fact: the human brain requires about 750 milliliters of blood per minute, about 15% of cardiac output," continued Blizz Kid, ignoring him. "Do you know how much blood those scientists' brains are getting right now? Zero, because their blood is frozen in place. Now, their brains are slowed down too, but not enough. They'll be fine for another minute, but after two minutes, at this rate, they risk permanent brain damage. After three, death."

Switch felt his body stiffen.

The villain eyed him cruelly, then took a step back toward the henchman holding the box. "This gizmo I pilfered might be something dangerous. Something puts all the people of Herald City in danger. Something worth doing whatever it takes to stop me from stealing it. *Maybe*," he said, patting the metal exterior. "But those scientists *will* die if they aren't rescued now."

"So you have a choice, Switch," he continued, looking Switch dead in the eye. "*Maybe* save the city, or *definitely* save the hostages. Which will it be?"

Switch hesitated for a moment. What should he do? What *could* he do? His time was up and he was powerless. He struggled to think of *how* he could either save the frozen scientists or recover the stolen equipment, let alone *which* he should do.

A mass of blue rushed past him toward the supervillain.

"*I choose both!*" bellowed Blue Eagle, rearing his fist back.

Blizz Kid stumbled backward, startled. His cocky expression melted away in an instant, a cry escaping his lips. He got his hands up just in time, creating a wall of ice between him and the incoming superhero. It protected him and his men from Blue Eagle's punch, but the force of the blow shattered the ice wall and sent the three of them sprawling to the floor. The box the henchmen was holding went tumbling to the ground.

Clay tossed the woman aside and went for the box.

Switch was quicker. He grabbed it and held it protectively in front of him as Clay pulled his magnum revolver. He aimed and put his finger over the trigger, then stopped as Switch crouched low, not giving him a clear shot.

"I know your limitations," he said, his teeth baring. "A bullet will kill you now."

"That's fine," said Switch, peeking out just over the box. "Shoot me and we can both die when you destroy this gizmo and your boss kills you for it. Wanna take that chance?"

There was a second of consideration before Clay huffed, lowering his weapon.

"Everyone! Forget the goods! Help me with Blue Eagle!" ordered Blizz Kid as he and his henchmen battled the superhero.

Blue Eagle dodged a beam of ice. "Switch, find a way to save those people!" he ordered. "I'll handle these lowlives."

"Got it!" acknowledged Switch. He quickly eyed the testing equipment in the room, looking for *anything* that could generate a flame.

All he saw was a couple of Bunsen burners. Not enough to melt the hard cube of ice that enveloped the research staff.

And time was running out.

"No gasoline and matches. No flamethrower. Are any of these acid?" he wondered frantically to himself, looking at the various chemicals in beakers and test tubes. His gaze moved down the long table....

....until he saw the tank of hydrogen at the end of it, with a hose funneling the hydrogen into an attached water tank.

He turned on the burners that lined the table as quickly as he could, then rushed to the hydrogen tank.

"I hope this works," he said to himself as he ripped the hose out and aimed it towards the flame.

Hydrogen escaped the hose right into the burner flames. The three flames combined just enough to reach the scientists. It wasn't much, but it was enough. Liquid water began to run down the ice as it started to melt.

Switch mentally pleaded with chemistry itself to work faster. He hoped the brain damage–or worse–that Blizz Kid talked about hadn't set in yet. He refused to let these people die.

He was so focused on rescuing them that he didn't notice Clay sneak up behind him until a hand grabbed his shoulder and spun him around. A fist landed just below his eye, sending him onto his back.

The hose danced around, spewing hydrogen gas everywhere.

Clay stood over him and aimed his magnum at the boy's head.

"Switch!" cried Blue Eagle, his battle with Blizz Kid not enough to distract him from his son's plight.

Behind him, Blizz Kid pointed. A sharp point of ice formed on his index fingertip. Blue Eagle's ears could just barely pick up the sound of such a small amount of water vapor crystalizing. Few people's could.

He was already moving before Blizz Kid fired the ice dart, grabbing the villain's wrist and pointing it at Clay's gun. The icicle pierced the magnum like a bullet, pinning it against the wall.

Effortlessly, Blue Eagle threw Blizz Kid across the room, sending the ice villain rolling across the floor toward the entrance. He positioned himself between the metal box and Blizz Kid as he watched him scramble to his feet.

"Everyone, retreat!" ordered Blizz Kid, backing out of the room.

"But if we don't get that box—" started one of the henchmen.

"If we stay and try to fight Blue Eagle, then it's jail or worse. So retreat!"

Blue Eagle started towards them, intending to take as many criminals into custody as possible, but the sound of gas hissing caught his attention. The hydrogen tank hose was still dancing like a snake under the control of an energetic charmer, and the scientists were still frozen.

Saving their lives took precedence over catching the bad guys.

No one noticed Jasper run from his spot behind the table. No one saw him rush toward the door after his fellow crooks. No one saw him turn around and watch what happened next in awe.

But he saw everything.

He saw Blue Eagle grab the hydrogen tank, which must have weighed hundreds of pounds, and pick it up like an empty school bag. He saw Blue Eagle run to the window and kick it, shattering the reinforced glass with one blow. He saw him hold the tank with one hand like a football and hurl it with the precision of a seasoned quarterback to a rooftop twenty blocks away, a rooftop that Blue Eagle could clearly see was empty. And he ran off just as he saw Blue Eagle turn and begin melting the ice holding the scientists with his eyebeams.

Minutes later, the female scientist that Clay had held hostage was being helped to her feet. "Are you okay, ma'am?" asked Blue Eagle.

She looked around in confusion. She had kept her head down and her eyes covered through it all, and was now surveying the aftermath of the battle. The window was broken and the hydrogen tank was gone. Her colleagues sat or stood huddled to one side of the room, soaking wet and panting hard. She just looked up at him, her eyes wordlessly asking all the questions her mind was having trouble putting to words.

"Everyone here is safe," reported the superhero, seeming to sense those exact questions. "Nothing was taken, and there is minimal damage."

His gaze shifted over to Switch, who was just getting to his feet. The young sidekick winced in pain as he held his blackened left eye.

The disapproving look on Blue Eagle's face was palpable. And Switch saw it. Recognized it all too well.

"I....we...." started the scientist, still too frazzled to even notice. She blinked a few times, the realization that it was over finally hitting her. "Thank you. Thank you both."

"It's all in a day's work, ma'am," said Blue Eagle, holding his disapproving glare.

Switch winced. And this time, it wasn't from his black eye.

Chapter 3

The door to the warehouse burst open, and in stomped Blizz Kid, followed by his men, including Jasper and Clay. Earlier, they had left in good spirits, expecting an easy job.

Now, their morale was gone, their hopes as empty as the warehouse.

"We are completely screwed. *Completely screwed*," said one of the henchmen, panic in his voice.

"Shut up," hissed Blizz Kid, nervously pacing back and forth as he kept his eyes focused on every nook and cranny of the old structure, as if scanning every spot for threats.

Jasper kept quiet, but certainly shared the guy's feelings. This was bad. They had failed in their job.

His gaze rested on a poster, old and faded. The smiling factory worker with his blue overalls and protective gear stood happily behind text that read, "A Safe Workplace Starts With YOU!"

A safe work environment was more of a fantasy to him than a flying pink unicorn that spit rainbows. He actually saw that once.

The henchman whimpered loudly. "She's gonna kill us. She's gonna *kill us!*"

"*Shut up!*" yelled Blizz Kid, a cloud of fine ice popping from his body like dust and settling to the ground. "She's not going to kill you. I will talk to her."

"And that is *all* you are going to do."

Everyone jumped at the sound of the female voice. It was soft, yet strong. Commanding. Matriarchal, with a hint of playfulness.

From the next room, a patch of grass that just grew out of the ground came into their view. The grass extended from one side of the door to the other. Flowers bloomed out of the grass despite the lack of soil on the warehouse floor. A thick tree trunk emerged just behind the wall, branches full of leaves hanging down from above.

The crooks' mouths were agape as a tiny garden—no, a *forest*—grew out of nothing from the concrete floor of a dead warehouse.

Vines covered the doorway like the swinging doors of an old saloon. They then parted, and she emerged.

She was a bizarre yet regal figure. Her green bodysuit had red vine designs that wrapped around her arms, legs, and torso, coming together in a chest insignia that appeared to be a heart at first, but on closer inspection, was the open mouth of a Venus Flytrap. White evening gloves covered her arms, and she wore the same color boots that reached almost to her knees.

Her face was completely hidden behind a mask of plant eyes. The outline of human eyes and a mouth gave off an unnerving feel, as if some*thing* rather than some*one* had them in her sights.

She adjusted her crown of thorns and tightened her hooded cloak, the dark green fabric extending behind her like a hero's cape.

"Don't think for a second that your ice will have any effect on my plants," she threatened. "Of course, if any of your men would like to test that, I'd be happy to give you a *fatal* demonstration."

One crook moved behind Jasper. "Wait, is that *Queen Venus*? We're working for *Queen Venus!?*" he whispered to Jasper, his widened eyes staring in horror at the villainess. "You guys picked me up as a last minute replacement. If I'd known...." his voice trailed off and he slowly shook his head.

One thug stepped forward. "Nuts to that, lady!" he yelled in anger. "I ain't gonna stand here while some broad too big for her bodysuit threatens me and my boss!"

"Randall, no!" said Blizz Kid.

While her eyes were hidden behind her mask, Jasper could see them narrow. He didn't know if she was sensitive about her slightly pudgy body or the attitude the man just gave her, but he could tell just by looking at her face that that angered her. And he couldn't see her face.

A trio of vines burst from the floor beneath Randall's feet, wrapping around his ankles, then his legs, then his torso and head until he was completely covered like a cocoon.

Jasper and the rest watched in horror as the cocoon shook back and forth as Randall struggled to escape, his muffled cries echoing throughout the room. They grew louder and more panicked, and yet seemed to become more distant.

No one tried to help him. No one even dared speak out and ask her to stop as he fell to the floor, squirming and shaking as he struggled to breathe.

"Now," said Queen Venus, impatience ever-present in her voice, "I expect you to deliver your report on how the job at the Herald City BioGenetics Research Lab went, without the misogyny or body shaming."

She paused to listen to Randall let out one final whimper. His movements ceased, the cocoon just laying on the floor as an inanimate tangle of plant pulp. "I hate closed minded bigots," she said.

There was a heavy silence among Blizz Kid and his men before Jasper finally whispered, "He's....dead."

"Of course he's dead. Randall was new in town and didn't know that this is Queen Venus, one of the most dangerous supervillains in the world and the archenemy of Blue Eagle and Switch," said Blizz Kid in a hushed voice. He stepped toward Queen Venus, his body on alert and his fingers slowly moving like a cowboy about to draw his pistol during a duel. "Me and the boys went to steal the device like you asked, but, ah, we were attacked by the Father-Son Duo.

They stopped us from completing the heist," he reported nervously. Quickly, he added, "I'm not going to ask for payment because we failed. We won't fail a second time."

Queen Venus paused, as if contemplating his answer. "Clay," she finally asked, "was the mission a success?"

Everyone turned in confusion to Clay, who gave a knowing smirk. "A hundred percent."

"What is going on here?" asked Blizz Kid in confusion.

"Mr. Clayton here is actually one of *my* henchmen," explained Queen Venus. A slight hint of triumph could be heard in her voice, pride that she had intellectually bested the other villain. "And he had a different mission than you."

"What do you mean?" he asked.

With a wide grin, Clay playfully smacked the back of Blizz Kid's neck. "Don't worry about it, buddy!" he said jovially, pinching his skin between his thumb and index finger.

The young supervillain shoved him away. "Touch me again," he threatened angrily, frost engulfing his fist, "and you will lose that hand!"

"That's enough, you two," cooed Queen Venus as if talking to a pair of rambunctious toddlers.

Blizz Kid glared at Clay for another second before waving the frost away. "What *was* his mission, anyway?" he asked, not taking his eyes off the henchman. "He didn't do anything but stand guard and menace the research staff."

"The answer will come to you eventually. But thanks to your efforts, I will soon become the ruler of Herald City," she said. "And not only will the people and their heroes not resist, but they will actively welcome me as their monarch."

"Why would they do that?" asked Blizz Kid, taken aback by such a bizarre claim. Queen Venus was a well known supervillain and feared by the public.

"You will do that, too."

"*Why* would I do that, too?"

She tilted her head, as if puzzled by someone questioning the obvious. "In the back of your mind, you already know the answer."

Jasper shuddered. He didn't like someone so powerful with such ill intent being so vague and mysterious.

But a job was a job, and this was how he earned his living.

"But now is not the time for such trivial questions," she quickly said. "The next phase of my operations is about to begin."

"What would you have us do?" asked Blizz Kid, gesturing to himself and his henchmen.

Queen Venus shook her head. "I will not arouse suspicion by using the same proxies twice. Don't think for a moment you are the only one of Blue Eagle's enemies I am utilizing." She nodded to someone unseen behind them. "You may show yourself now."

Jasper jumped at the sudden sound of paper rustling behind them. What he saw made his blood run cold.

The man on the workplace safety poster has changed. He was still smiling, but his eyes were now narrowed in a focused glare. His mouth then began to move, extending into a wide grin.

Frozen in fear, Jasper watched as the man flicked the safety message away, the letters disappearing somewhere "behind" the poster. He then reached out of the paper, gripping the walls as he stepped out into the real world.

As he did, he physically changed. His protective clothing disappeared, replaced with a red costume with white cape, gloves, and boots, a darker red mask just covering his eyes, and a white vertical rectangle on his chest. He himself was now literally a different person, a teenage boy with scraggly red hair that reached down to his shoulder blades.

But his expression never changed. It was one of cruel excitement and expectation.

Jasper stepped back. All the henchmen except for Clay stepped back, instinctively not wanting to be near the uncanny, seemingly paranormal display.

Only Blizz Kid stood his ground, watching dispassionately, completely unimpressed, as the figure stepped forward.

"I trust you know what to do, *Poster Boy*," said Queen Venus.

Poster Boy nodded and clasped his hands together. "*Finally*. It's my turn now."

Chapter 4

Switch was forlorn as he entered his bedroom. His father was behind him. Both were still in costume.

"....and you *should* be embarrassed, Jack! I would be if I performed that poorly today," Blue Eagle was finishing.

Switch just held his glazed over expression. He had been listening to this for the better part of an hour.

"Sit down," commanded Blue Eagle.

Switch did as he was told, stifling a sigh as he sat down on the bed. Blue Eagle stood over him.

"You did absolutely horrible out there during the lab rescue," he admonished.

"I know," murmured Switch apologetically, his eyes lowered.

"Oh, *you know*? I'm glad you do," said Blue Eagle. He leaned against the wall, taking care not to rest his hand against one of Switch's metal band posters. "Jack, tell me exactly what you did wrong. Right now. I want to make sure *you know*."

Switch winced internally. He actually didn't quite know what he did wrong. He knew that he utterly failed to rescue the scientists and stop Blizz Kid, but the exact error in judgment he made eluded him. It was a hectic situation where it just seemed like everything was going wrong, and he had been lacking in time and options.

"I....shouldn't have used a hydrogen flamethrower to melt frozen people....?" was his eventual answer. He hoped that it was the answer that his father was looking for.

The look on Blue Eagle's face told him it wasn't.

"You have strength, speed, flight, and eyebeams, yet you chose to engage a room full of criminals with guns and *hostages* with invulnerability. A power only good for defending *yourself*," replied Blue Eagle in exasperation.

"What power should I have used?"

Blue Eagle shook his head. "Jack, I can't answer that for you," he said. "You just turned 15 and you've been doing this since you were 12. You need to be able to choose the right power for any given situation."

"It's harder than you think," complained Switch. "You don't have to deal with that because your strength, flight, senses, and eyebeams are ready at all times."

"Tell that to the people you fail to save, Jack!" snapped his father. "Tell their families that you couldn't save their loved ones because it was 'harder than they think'. I'm sure that will be of great comfort to them."

There was no use in arguing, and Switch regretted even trying. He usually never did. Usually these lectures ended quicker if he just stayed quiet and apologized.

This one hit hard because his father was right about that point. It didn't matter how *hard* not having reliable superpowers was. A life or death situation was just that regardless.

"Now, you're absolutely right, Jack. I *don't* have to deal with what you deal with. Only being able to use one power at a time. Having it shut off randomly after two to five minutes after activating it. Having a cooldown period of a minute or two before being able to activate another one," continued Blue Eagle. He stood straight and folded his arms. "Tough. You *do* have to deal with that. And that means you are going to have to work harder and figure out how to deal with it if you want to be a superhero."

Those words stung. Ever since his powers developed at 10 years old, they had never been reliable. Other superheroes had the full suite of whatever superpowers they had available at all times, but not Switch. It was always that way and there was nothing he could do about it. It wasn't a question of not training hard enough or anything like that. Those were just his limitations.

They were a real sore spot for him. It wasn't his fault. It was just how his powers were.

Blue Eagle raised an eyebrow as he suddenly noticed the open laptop on Switch's bed, left where it was when it came time to leap into action.

"What's this? 'A New Way To Fight Crime: Social Justice, Rehabilitation, and Crime Prevention'," he read. His face crinkled in bewilderment. "What *is* this nonsense?"

"Just an article I was reading," said Switch self-consciously, quickly picking up the laptop to look at the screen as if he didn't know what Blue Eagle was talking about.

"Maybe instead of thinking about how to treat criminals like the biggest victims on Earth, you should be thinking about how to put them away for good."

"I am! Um...." Switch wrecked his brain trying to remember some of what he read. He found the arguments for social justice and better treatment of criminals compelling, airtight. So why was he fumbling to actually push back on something wrong his father said? "It's just.... It's a fact that being tough doesn't work. Studies show....studies show the best way to deal with criminals is to give money to programs so they don't want to be criminals, or don't need to be criminals, because poverty can make people criminals."

He cringed internally. The video essays he watched online explained it way better.

Blue Eagle scoffed. "I'm sure poverty is what makes Wave Runner a criminal, what with his advanced equipment. Or Music Major and Music Minor," he said dismissively. He shook his head. "Criminal rehabilitation? No, the only thing that will rehabilitate someone like Gravitational Paul is for everyone to start being tough on crime. Maybe give these guys a good old fashioned sock in the jaw. That's how things were back when your grandfather was a superhero, that's how things were for most of my career, and that's how we do things because that's what works."

"I know, but...." Switch paused. "If I want to have a solo career soon, I'll have to do things my own way."

"With the way you've been going lately? "Blue Eagle shook his head. "You're not going to have a solo career any time soon. At this rate, you'll only ever be a sidekick."

He turned and left the room, his disappointment still hanging in the air like steam from a pipe. Those words stayed with Switch, piercing him in a way that even his invulnerability couldn't protect him from. With a sigh, he fell backward onto his bed, staring up at the ceiling and watching his dream of becoming a great superhero fade away.

Chapter 5

Jasper's footsteps could be heard from halfway down the hall, if anyone was there to listen. The old stairwell creaked and groaned, seemingly as tired as he was.

He stepped into the decrepit hallway, ignoring the peeling paint and stained floor as he strode with both excitement and exhaustion toward the second door on the left. Pulling a key out of his pocket, he unlocked it and entered.

"Carla? Babe, I'm home!" he called, entering the apartment. He pulled an envelope out of the pocket of his jacket, which he hung on a hook nailed into the wall. With a smile on his face, he walked toward the kitchen. "I got paid for the job! I almost didn't, but—Ah, it's a long story. But it's enough that we can finally pay off that Charlemagne Family scum...."

He felt the blood drain from his face when he entered the kitchen.

At the table sat his wife, Carla. The light skinned black woman sat frozen, a look of forced calm just barely holding in utter terror. Also at the table was their six year old daughter, Rosa, coloring in her coloring book.

And between them sat a lanky man with slicked back hair wearing a half open buttoned down shirt, a light sports coat, and a smug smile. Behind him, in the corner, stood a burly red hair man in a white turtleneck and black vest.

"Honey," said Carla through a forced smile, "we have guests."

Rosa looked up, excited to see her father. "Daddy, we have guests!" she exclaimed giddily, sitting up. "This man is really nice and says he helped us out and wants you to help him out!"

"I see that," said Jasper, trying to keep an even face as he looked back and forth between his daughter and the man that sat next to her. "Rosa, sweetie, why don't you go to your room, okay? Go to your room."

"Now now, Jasper. You need to ask me for permission to let folks come and go," said the man, his voice smooth like a shady salesman's. He gave him a knowing look. "And that's just a fraction of what you owe me."

With a sharp breath, Jasper turned his attention toward the man. "Please, Mickey," he pleaded in a quiet voice so as not to scare Rosa, "let my six year old daughter not be in the room for this."

The man, Mickey, thought for a moment. "I've proven my point," he finally said with a nod.

Jasper turned to his daughter. "Rosa, go to your room," he told her. "Daddy has to talk to our guest for a few minutes."

Rosa nodded and closed her coloring book. She held onto it as she got up and reached up to give her father a hug. He kneeled down to embrace her, giving her a kiss on the forehead. Afterward, she gathered her crayons and left down the hall, into her bedroom.

As her door closed, Jasper started, "Listen, Mickey, I—"

"Sit," interrupted Mickey, nodding to the empty chair near Jasper.

There was a pause as a million emotions seemed to hit Jasper at once. But, like a well trained dog, he obeyed the command to sit.

"Jasper, I like you. You seem like a good man. An *honest* man," said Mickey. "So I hope you understand that you can't escape paying back the money you borrowed. I've come to collect the first installment."

"I wasn't avoiding anything, and I ain't about to try to get one over on the Charlemagne Family," assured Jasper. "I borrowed $1,000 because I needed it. My family needed it. And now I have more than just the first installment."

He held the envelope up in front of him and then carefully placed it on the table, as if trying not to spook an animal. "There. That's $1,500. The full amount, plus 50% interest."

Mickey eyed the envelope, then Jasper. He gave a short chuckle. "You misunderstand how finance works outside the banks and all those regulated institutions," he said. "You see, when a lender loans money, they charge interest based on a risk assessment of you, the borrower. And you, Jasper, are a very risky borrower, so they charge a high interest rate."

"I know how loans work," said Jasper, keeping his voice as steely as he could without it being disrespectful.

He was also trying not to sound like he was scared out of his mind. What was Mickey getting at?

"If you know that, then you should know that loans need servicing, and that it's common practice for lenders to charge a service fee," continued Mickey. The corners of his mouth curled even more upward. "And we're charging you a service fee of $2,000."

Jasper's jaw dropped. "That's insane!" he shouted. He glanced down the hall toward Rosa's room, then spoke again with a lower voice. "A service fee? C'mon, Mickey. I'm done! I just paid off the loan, and I won't pay a penny more!"

"That's your choice, but it means you'll be getting a visit from the Family's debt collectors," said Mickey nonchalantly, jerking a thumb toward the large man standing behind him. With a cruel grin, he rubbed the back of his hand across Carla's cheek. "If they can't collect from you, they'll collect from your wife. Or your daughter."

Carla shivered, but otherwise kept still and quiet even as his finger caressed her cheek.

Mickey turned his attention back toward Jasper. "How much money did you say you took in?"

Jasper nodded toward the envelope on the table. "That's $1,500 right there."

"Is that it?" asked Mickey, menacingly leaning forward.

Despite his jaw tightening and the sudden numb feeling in his hands and shoulders from anger, Jasper kept a submissive countenance. "There's another $1,500 in my coat."

Mickey nodded, then gestured toward the large man to go get it. Everyone was silent as the enforcer disappeared for a moment into the apartment entrance, and reappeared a moment later with another envelope.

"Very good, Jasper. Very good," said Mickey, inspecting both envelopes. "I see about $3,000 in cash. That covers the service fee, an early principal payment fee, and the first installment. Congratulations, your principal is down to $900."

He stood up and adjusted his sports coat. "I'll be back soon for your next installment payment," he informed Jasper. "Until then...." He nodded to both of them and then gestured to the enforcer to follow them. Together, the two Charlemagne Family mobsters walked out of the kitchen and out of the apartment.

There was a heavy silence that hung in the air as Jasper and Carla sat there, stunned by what just happened. It took a moment before one of them could even speak.

"We have to find another way to come up with that money," she finally said.

"We did come up with the money," whimpered Jasper, crestfallen. His gaze rested on a random spot on the tablecloth pattern.

"You didn't. Not in a way that would satisfy those mobster creeps. We still owe."

"We don't owe," said Jasper, shaking his head. "I just paid in full, plus interest."

"That doesn't matter. The loan shark said—"

Jasper's fists pounded the table, causing the salt and pepper shakers to spill. "I don't care what he said! I paid! You saw it!"

"I know! I saw!" she shouted back at him. "I also just saw that loan shark say that payment essentially didn't count! And now we have to come up with more money. Lots more."

"That's not fair! I did everything right! I did the job at the research lab. I got the money we owe and more!"

"That's not how this works. Right now, they control our lives, they control our finances, and they control how much we owe. We owe what they say we owe. And right now, you've got to find a way to make the next payment or we're in trouble."

Jasper let out an exasperated sigh, plopping his forehead into his palms.

"I'm doing what I can to help," continued Carla. "But there are only so many shifts I can pick up at the store or the restaurant, and we can't afford a babysitter. And I can't keep taking Rosa to work with me at the Moodoo Burger. So you have to figure out a way."

"What more money can I get?" wailed Jasper into his palms. "I wanted to get out of this line of work, but now I'm in it for the long haul?"

"We knew this was a possibility when we decided to borrow money from the mob."

He gave a sharp laugh as his head shot up. "'Decided'? This was never a *voluntary* decision. We need money for food! Rent! Rosa's medicine! And there aren't too many ways for me to earn money."

"Well, find a way!" she shouted. She shot to her feet. "Neither of us can get a good paying job, but you can't get *anything* because of your criminal record! So if you have to be a henchman for one of those villains to protect your six year old daughter from the mob, then you do it!"

He said nothing as she turned to leave the kitchen. She paused at the door and turned around.

"I understand you were dealt a bad hand, but you need to do something about it other than sitting there and blaming society or whatever else for your problems," she told him. Her voice was low, direct, and sharp as an arrow. "If you don't show respect for yourself, no one else will."

She left him with those words. And he sat there, staring at the tablecloth, wondering how things could have gone so wrong when he did everything right.

Chapter 6

Workers scurried about the auditorium, setting up lights and putting up posters and banners. One worker set up a podium on stage, and behind him, another was affixing a banner that read "Liberty Park Opportunity Project".

Next to the podium, Blue Eagle and Switch were talking to Herald City Mayor Michael Warren and the Herald City Chief of Police.

Or at least, Blue Eagle was. Switch's presence wasn't *needed* per se. But as the sidekick son of a patriotic superhero, he made a great prop for "family values".

"I'm very glad you're able to stand by me for this event," the mayor told the heroes. The sound of a mic boom drew his attention for a brief second toward the worker setting it up at the podium. He turned back to Blue Eagle. "I couldn't ask Mr. America or Lady Liberty to be up here as they're government-affiliated and neither SPIRE nor any other agency can be seen as supporting or opposing local government policy."

"It's one of the perks of being an independent superhero," said Blue Eagle. "You're free to support whatever cause you want."

Warren nodded, then turned to Switch. "What about you, Switch? Have you found yourself getting passionate about any particular causes lately?"

There were so many answers Switch wanted to give. Social justice and criminal rehabilitation were the two that immediately came to mind. But then he remembered his conversation with his father the other day after the lab mission.

Biting his tongue, he simply answered, "Not really."

"That's a shame," said Warren. "So many young people your age are finding themselves more involved in politics and social advocacy."

"We're pretty apolitical," said Blue Eagle. "Though I'm always a firm believer of tough policing and harsh sentencing for criminals."

"You always have been," said Warren with a laugh, patting him on the shoulder. He leaned forward and said quietly, "That's why I can always count on you to make a statement in support of our police. Mr. America is too much of a lib. He won't do it."

Blue Eagle chuckled, then asked, "Are you going to reiterate the need for Herald City to be tough on crime during your speech?"

"I will be," said the Police Chief. He frowned as he looked around at the Liberty Park Opportunity Project all around the auditorium. "I'm not a fan of his so-called revitalization project you have going on, Warren," he said in his usual gruff demeanor, "but any chance to put forward to the press the need for more police officers is one I'm happy to take."

As Warren opened his mouth to respond, the worker from the podium came up to the Chief. "Sir, I'm just about done setting up the mic, and I just have to put one last piece behind your collar."

The Chief looked at the podium and frowned. "Isn't the mic over there?"

The worker flashed an irreverent look at him. "The mic's volume control is a little iffy, so this is a piece that connects to your collar that acts as a second mic if the sound ain't carrying."

The Chief nodded, and the worker placed a small plastic device that looked like a band for headphones behind his collar.

"Anyway," said Warren, turning his attention back to their conversation, "tonight's speech isn't about that—the crime, I mean. It's to promote the new construction project at Liberty Park."

Switch started to tune out their conversation. It wasn't interesting to him, and the whole reason that they were here was stupid. Not the part where they provide protection for the mayor, of course. There was a solid 5 to 7% chance that some supervillain would attempt to abduct or kill him. Possibly one of Blue Eagle's villains, like Blizz Kid.

Or their archnemesis, Queen Venus.

No, it was the reason that this event was being held that he thought was stupid. Breaking ground in Liberty Park—a massive sprawling park with a nature preserve, zoo, and monuments—to build an office skyscraper was just stupid.

He wanted to tell the mayor how stupid it was, but he knew Warren wouldn't listen. And his dad would probably get angry for showing such disrespect.

Blue Eagle really was a product of his time. And his generation, the Silver Age of Heroism. That was two, perhaps three generations of heroes ago, and many have retired over the last few years.

His gaze aimlessly wandered toward the posters and banners selling the project. Smiling office workers from royalty-free image websites took center stage on posters promising more jobs, more business, less crime, and more growth. As far as he was concerned, they were nothing but propaganda posters made to sell the idea of destroying part of a park to make more money for greedy billionaires.

Then his attention turned toward the worker who was just finishing up clipping the mic onto the Chief.

Switch couldn't place it, but there was something familiar about the man's face. He was somewhere in his twenties or thirties, bald with tattoos. Switch thought they looked like the symbols of militant bigoted groups, but he didn't want to say anything just in case he was wrong. The man had a short goatee that was neatly cut. His lips were pressed and his eyes had a resentful or malicious glint in them.

There was a brief instance where they locked eyes. That malicious glint seemed to intensify in that instant, as if he knew something Switch didn't.

Switch didn't like the man. He felt put off by him. But he couldn't place the face. Who was he?

There was something about the way he seemed to pinch the back of the Chief's neck between his index finger and thumb that made the hairs on the back of Switch's own neck stand up.

The way the man touched the Chief's neck, even *that* seemed familiar.

The Chief seemed oblivious to the man, whose presence he had seemingly forgotten about as he listened to the mayor continue droning on about the Liberty Park construction project.

"It has low public approval," Warren was telling Blue Eagle, "but the audience will be filled with representatives from the construction industry who will be quite happy with my commitment to infrastructure projects."

"Those funds would be better allocated to law enforcement in the most super-crime-ridden city in the world," said the Chief gruffly, running a hand through his graying hair. He turned to the worker.

"Are you done yet, man? It doesn't take this long to set up a mic."

"I just finished, sir."

The Chief grunted. "Maybe if you'd stop caressing my neck like we're dating, you'd have done your job faster."

The worker didn't say anything. He just gave the Chief a knowing glance that Switch didn't like.

"Now, be nice, Chief," said Warren. "And you should be supporting this, Chief. This will bring more jobs to Herald City. And more jobs equals less crime."

"More cops equals less crime," said the Chief.

At any other time, Switch would have needed superstrength to resist the urge to say something. All the reading and watching online videos on the topic told him that jobs for already-wealthy white collar workers and streets flooded with cops wouldn't reduce crime. Decreasing income inequality would. But nobody ever seemed to even entertain such a notion. It was common sense once he watched a couple of video essays about it.

Right now, though, his attention was on that worker. That look he gave the Chief bothered him. The inability to place the face bothered him.

Ignorant of this, Warren glanced over at a few people in professional attire who entered the auditorium, greeted by other similarly dressed people.

"If you'll excuse me, I must meet with some members of the construction industry association that just walked in," he said. He clasped Blue Eagle's hand. "Blue Eagle, thank you for coming."

"Always a pleasure, sir."

Switch was focused on the worker who had quickly and quietly left through a backstage exit when the mayor's hand—offered as a handshake—snapped him back to reality.

"Switch, always good to see you," he said.

"I—uh, thanks," stammered Switch as he shook his hand.

With that, Warren turned to greet the newcomers. Blue Eagle gently nudged Switch's shoulder.

"We should head to the back with everyone else that's going to be invited onstage," he suggested.

They walked down the hallway of the government building, past posters that reminded people of civil rights they had, benefit programs they were entitled to, and government jobs they could apply for, local, state, and federal alike. All of them had smiling people on them, either sighing with exaggerated relief or standing with their hands on their hips and a confident expression on their faces.

For some reason, one poster near a vending machine caught Switch's eye that read "*No powers? NO PROBLEM! You can still be super! SPIRE is hiring for support roles today!*"

He scoffed internally. It felt almost like the ad was intended for him. As if *he* would ever become an employee of some big US superhero intelligence agency that was probably violating someone's civil rights at that very moment.

Ignoring it, he and Blue Eagle headed to the room they were expected to wait in before they would be called onstage.

C: *"the jobs dun. quuens got wat she wanted from me"*

PB: "*Excellent. First part of the job is complete. No one noticed?*"

C: "*no1. those eagle supes r here, but they saw nutyin*"

C: "*nuthin**"

PB: "*Good, then the actual mission is complete. Time for the show to start!*"

C: "*I m cumin back too the car. u have it ready to go?*"

JC: "*The engine's rubbing.*"

JC: "*Running**"

C: "*good man. i knew u couldnt stay away from dis life, buddy*"

C: "*lol think about ur lady later. now we wait 4 pb 2 do his thing. not that it matters, tho. we already got the mayor. and now the chief 2.*"

PB: "*It matters. A good show is necessary to keep those prying eyes off of us. And I'll give them the show of a lifetime!*"

Clay figured that was enough. He didn't have time to do a text chain back-and-forth right now. They'd be in the car together in a few minutes.

But everyone in that auditorium was about to get one heck of a scare.

He grinned. He got to the Chief and did what he had to do without issue. For a second, it had seemed that Blue Eagle's sidekick had recognized him, but apparently not.

He loved the danger of being a criminal.

But even he was going to stay out of the way of what happened next.

Switch sat bored in the conference room with Blue Eagle and a few other city officials and business leaders. He was bored and waiting for their cue to head for the stage. Mayor Warren was about to start his speech, and soon he would announce them to come stand with him in a show of support for this construction initiative.

He wasn't happy about having to be there, but Blue Eagle insisted. So he sat in silence and waited for his cue to go stand in silence.

Feeling a sense of boredom-induced hunger, he got to his feet. "I'm just gonna run and grab a quick snack from the vending machine," he told his father, starting toward the door.

"Be quick," said Blue Eagle, pointing to the TV screen where the mayor was approaching the podium and shaking a woman's hand. "Mayor Warren's speech is about to start. We're expected to be onstage in about five minutes."

"Don't worry," said Switch sarcastically. "I've got superspeed."

Blue Eagle just chuckled in response as his son left the room.

Switch walked quickly but without any enhanced speed down the hallway toward the vending machine they passed earlier.

He took a minute to look over the choices of chips and candy. As he reached toward his belt to pull out some cash, he suddenly felt uneasy.

Something was different. Something was *wrong*.

But what? Nothing seemed to have changed. Everything was where it should be, yet felt off somehow. It was like arriving home to find everything had been moved two inches to the left.

He blinked and looked around. The hallway was empty, but there wasn't exactly a crowd before. Plus, everyone was in the auditorium.

The snacks looked normal. He recognized the brand names. The posters were all where they were before. Presumably at least. He recognized the text for the SPIRE—

The person on the SPIRE recruitment ad was gone.

The people on *all* the posters nearby were gone.

The words were still there, but the *people* in them were gone.

Switch blinked to make sure what he was seeing was real. It was.

He stared in disbelief. What could make the people in the posters—

His eyes went wide. "Oh no!" he exclaimed.

He broke into a run toward the auditorium, hoping not to see what he thought he would see.

His heart sank when he arrived. It was exactly what he thought he would see.

It was chaos and pandemonium as people ran for their lives. The large posters were a surreal sight to see.

The smiling office workers featured in them were pulling themselves out of the posters, shrinking to normal human heights as they landed on the floor. They rose to their feet.

On the stage, the last of the mayor's bodyguards was just getting knocked out by a person in a red costume. Multiple clones of that person stood over other defeated bodyguards.

It was Poster Boy, one of the most dangerous—and deranged—supervillains in Blue Eagle's Rogues Gallery.

There were now two dozen Poster Boy clones in the auditorium as the royalty free office worker characters morphed into clones as well.

Together, a sinister smile spread across their faces as they turned toward the stage and menacingly made their way toward the mayor.

Chapter 7

Five clones of Poster Boy surrounded the mayor on the stage. Nearly two dozen others were in the auditorium aisles.

All wore the same foul grin.

"Mayor Michael Warren," said the leader of the five on stage as the mayor backed away in fear, "you're coming with *us*."

A red beam slammed into his chest like a bullet, knocking him off his feet. Before he could land on his back, he faded away. The clone had disappeared from existence. There wasn't so much as a wisp of smoke left.

The other clones turned in shock—then anger—at the source of the beam.

"Gasp! *Poster Boy?* Trying to kidnap the mayor?" jeered Switch with fake surprise as the red glow around his eyes faded. "Well I *never*!"

"As a matter of fact, I *am* trying to kidnap the mayor," replied another clone, echoing Switch's tone. His lips curled upward. "Killing you is a bonus, though. You!" he slapped the shoulder of the clone next to him. "Attack Switch! Clip this little birdie's wings!"

The other clone rushed toward Switch, who didn't move at all. Instead, the sidekick folded his arms, a confident smirk resting on his face.

Another eyebeam hit the charging poster clone in the chest, causing him to get knocked back and vanish.

Switch turned with muted surprise. That wasn't him, but he wasn't at all surprised to see his father enter onto the stage, the red glow fading from his eyes.

"Gasp! *Poster Boy?* Trying to kidnap the mayor?" he said, a mocking smirk on his face that could only come from a dad telling a lame joke. He placed his hand theatrically over his heart. "Well I *never*!"

"Sorry, Blue Eagle. I already said that," said Switch.

"Really?"

Switch nodded. "Word for word."

Blue Eagle snapped his fingers in mock disappointment. "And here I thought you'd let your old man be the one to snark," he said.

"You two have mocked me for the last time," growled Poster Boy. "I have you outnumbered."

"You always have us outnumbered," countered Blue Eagle, his eyes glowing red. Switch's followed suit.

The poster clones rushed the stage, but the Father-Son Duo held their ground, firing eyebeams at each one. One after the other, the poster clones vanished, defeated easily by the heroes.

It took only a few moments, but all the poster clones were defeated, leaving only one instance of Poster Boy—likely the real Poster Boy given that he was the one giving orders to the rest—to face down Blue Eagle and Switch.

"Now we have *you* outnumbered," said Switch.

The doors to the auditorium suddenly burst open. Dozens and dozens of clones of Poster Boy—all generated from posters elsewhere in the building and outside—rushed in, letting out a collective cry as they rushed toward the heroes and into battle.

"You were saying?" replied the real Poster Boy over the sound of his endless army, a triumphant grin spreading across his face.

"Ahh, shoot," was all Switch could say in response as he watched more and more of poster clones pour into the building.

Without hesitation, Blue Eagle pushed off his feet, flying through the air towards one of the approaching columns of poster clones with both hands spread out in front of him. It was an impressive display of strength and momentum as clones flew into the air like bowling pins as he barreled through them.

"Switch! Remember that, individually, his poster clones are frail and weak! And they lack the individuality and sentience that makes ordinary humans alive!" he reminded his son as he punched and threw away clone after clone after clone. "There's no need to hold back, and they're easy to kill!"

"I'm aware of that," muttered Switch dryly as he eyebeamed three of them in quick succession. Did his father really think he didn't know how to fight Poster Boy? He immediately regretted his rude tone, mainly because it was possible that Blue Eagle's super hearing allowed him to hear that.

Poster Boy laughed. "Individually, my poster clones may be weak. But together, they are strong enough for me to be considered one of the most dangerous villains in your Rogues Gallery!"

The battle continued, with Blue Eagle fighting off one column of clones right in the aisle, and Switch blasting away at the other as they rushed the stage.

Blue Eagle kicked one poster clone so hard it crashed into the ceiling, disappearing from existence as was the case when they defeated one of them. The same thing happened when he hit another in the face with enough force to dent a steel beam, only a fraction of his might.

Switch backed up as the clones started getting closer to the stage. He blasted away three in rapid succession as two managed to get to him, surrounding him. One threw a wide punch which Switch ducked, hitting the other one and causing it to vanish. Switch grabbed the remaining attacker by the cape and threw him into the rest just as they got to the stage, knocking all of them back. He then let loose with his eyebeams, blasting them all as they struggled to get up and maneuver around each other.

A poster clone leapt onto Blue Eagle's back, applying a tight sleeper hold. Blue Eagle didn't even react to it as he grabbed two more by their hair and slammed their foreheads together. He grabbed the one hanging off his neck and flew into the air.

"Got an early Christmas present for you, Switch!" exclaimed Blue Eagle as he threw the clone in Switch's direction. The poster clone disappeared upon taking an eyebeam from Switch directly in the back.

Mayor Warren stood in awe as he watched the battle unfold before him. Poster Boy's clones were like toddlers before the Father-Son Duo.

Two suited bodyguards came up beside him. "Sir, we have a car ready in the back," informed one of them, nudging the mayor's shoulder.

Warren nodded and, taking one last look at the battle, hurried with his men out of the room.

Switch glanced back at the mayor leaving. He should have felt relief that he was safe, but he didn't. He turned back and continued firing his eyebeams at the poster clones, but a part of his mind went right back to the two suited bodyguards.

Something felt off about them.

He knew he didn't have much time left before his powers disappeared. His mind needed to focus on the column of poster clones that he was keeping at bay. There were so many, all coming from the various posters in the lobby and right outside the building that Poster Boy was able to reuse over and over.

It then suddenly dawned on him. He remembered that he knew what was going on because of the posters in the hallways backstage. Where the mayor had been whisked away to.

And no poster clones were coming from that direction.

His stomach dropped, and he whirled around and sprinted backstage.

"Switch! Get back–!" started Blue Eagle just as a group of poster clones dived on him, only to be thrown in all directions by a sudden burst of the superhero's strength.

It was a very short run to the building's back entrance. The sound of Mayor Warren's loud demands to be let go led the way for Switch. He slammed the door open and took less than a second to survey the scene. Out of sight from the general public was a car waiting behind the building.

The two bodyguards were forcing Mayor Warren into the car.

Switch didn't hesitate. He eyebeamed the would-be kidnappers in the back. They vanished into nothing.

"Just as I thought. Poster clones," he said to himself.

The front passenger door opened. Clay exited and stood with a look of apathetic confidence. Almost like he had enough but was still going to have some fun.

Undeterred, Switch looked him up and down. "You a poster clone?"

"Nope. I'm a real man, little boy," replied Clay with a chuckle.

Switch nodded. "Mmhmm. makes sense since a poster clone would not be able to drive the mayor all the way out of town because it would be too far away from the actual Poster Boy."

He still couldn't shake the familiarity of Clay's face. But then his gaze shifted over to the driver.

Sitting behind the wheel, Jasper felt his stomach tighten into a knot. Or was it a noose? He fought the urge to step on the gas and get the heck away from there. He needed the money, but this was about to get so much worse.

The superhero and the driver locked eyes for a moment, and then it suddenly became clear to Switch.

"Wait, I recognize you both. You were at the lab. Blizz Kid's henchmen," he said, his eyes widening with recognition. He turned his focus toward Clay. "You were the one who gave me the black eye."

His eyes glowed red, hiding a cold glare.

"Let me return the favor," he said, widening his eyes, a reflexive movement to fire his eyebeams.

His eyebeams didn't fire.

His eyes twitched, but the crimson red blast that was supposed to burst out and slam into Clay's chest, knocking him out, never came.

Instead, Switch stood there frozen, realizing that his powers just entered cooldown and he would have to wait at least a minute to use them again.

Clay laughed. "What's up, little man? Your powers having performance issues?" He moved toward the car door, crouching slightly and holding his hand out toward Jasper. "Gun."

"W-what?" stuttered Jasper.

"This is the part where I make a real name for myself by killing Blue Eagle's sidekick," elaborated Clay, never taking his eyes off Switch. He waved his fingers toward Jasper. "*Gun.*"

Switch backed away. He was powerless against an armed assailant without his powers, too far away to land a surprise hit on Clay, and too small to survive in a fight against this man for the two minutes he needed for his powers to recharge.

Only one thing left to do.

"Mr. Mayor! Back inside!" he ordered, quickly turning around to run inside.

He stopped when he saw two Poster Boy clones standing in the doorway that led back inside. There was an instant where they flashed ear to ear grins before suddenly slamming the door shut, locking Switch and Warren outside.

Outside with an armed man who was not too squeamish to kill a 15 year old.

Switch turned around to see a grin on Clay's face.

"Sorry, kid. You ain't goin' nowhere," he said. Without looking back, he tapped the seat. "Clemens, *gun.*"

"Yeah!.... Sorry, yeah!" was Jasper's reply. He quickly reached into the glove compartment and pulled out a pistol.

He turned and looked at Switch, and there was a brief moment where the two locked eyes. Jasper's skin was pale, and Switch could see it. The man's jaw hung open, as if he were looking for someone to ask for help desperately.

He had been in the henchman business for years, but he was never prone to violence. He usually stayed out of the fights and was assigned support roles, such as driver. And he *never* tussled with superheroes. Hiding was always the way to go.

He had been arrested a couple times, but nothing ever really stuck. Harmless small fry, that's what he was.

And now Clay wanted him to directly participate in the murder of a teenage boy.

Superhero or not, Jasper couldn't do it.

Clay's eyes were still on Switch. Quickly and silently, Jasper removed the mag and the chambered round, sliding the gun back into a fire-ready position, and shoving the magazine and bullet under him.

"Here, sorry," he said, handing the unloaded weapon to Clay.

"'Bout time," said Clay with a slight hint of frustration in his voice.

Switch kept his face even. He saw Jasper unload the weapon, and he saw that Clay didn't know. He didn't know what to think about Jasper, but that could come later.

Gun or no gun, Clay was a dangerous man. And without his powers, Clay was a threat to both him and Mayor Warren.

He narrowed his eyes and focused on Clay's. "Go ahead. Do it," he dared menacingly. "It will be the worst mistake of your life."

Clay's eyebrows raised, clearly amused and enjoying the situation.

"Everyone makes mistakes," he said, his words hanging lightly with the air of philosophical reflection. He closed one eye and aimed the pistol right between Switch's eyes. "The question is how will you be remembered for yours."

There was a tense pause before Clay pulled the trigger. The gun clicked empty.

"What?" breathed the ruthless gangster, fruitlessly pulling the trigger a few more times. "I thought I loaded this thing before we came out here!"

As Clay instinctively inspected the gun, Switch made his move. He rushed toward Clay, grabbing the man's wrist with one hand and punching him in the jaw with the other.

Without his powers, Switch wasn't particularly strong. He was in good shape and wasn't *weak*, but was a slim boy and wasn't all that much of a fighter. Clay, on the other hand, was a hardened criminal who had gotten into more than his share of fights.

He was used to punches in the face. The man grabbed Switch by the shoulders and kneed him hard in the gut, sending the superhero crumpling to his knees.

"I might not be able to shoot you, kid," said Clay, kneeling down to pick up the gun that had fallen from his hands during the exchange. He rubbed his jaw, feeling the back of his teeth with his tongue. Gripping the barrel of the gun, he stood over Switch, who grunted in pain as he held his stomach. He raised the weapon and prepared to beat Switch with the butt of the gun. "But I can still kill you. And I assure you that you're gonna feel a *lot* of pain."

The door burst open. Poster Boy quickly shut it behind him and ran toward the car.

"Get in the car!" he shouted frantically.

"Why? What happened?" asked Clay.

"Start the car! Forget the mayor! We're leaving!" yelled Poster Boy, rushing toward the rear passenger door, sprinting in a desperate attempt to escape something horrible behind him.

The door burst open again, this time flying off its hinges. The two poster clones that had been standing guard sailed through the air, disappearing forever before ever hitting the ground.

From the chaos and carnage came Blue Eagle, shooting out of the doorway like a cannonball. He shoulder tackled Poster Boy, sending the villain crashing into the trunk of the car.

Clay scrambled into the passenger seat just as Jasper, screaming frantically, shifted the car into drive and stomped on the gas pedal. The tires squealed as the vehicle peeled out, turning a corner while Clay's legs were still dangling outside as he scrambled to get in.

Blue Eagle didn't bother to go after the two henchmen. Not when the more important figures in this incident were right here.

"Are you okay?" he asked Switch, offering his hand to help him up.

"Yeah, I'm good," grunted Switch, still holding his aching stomach as his father helped him to his feet.

A disapproving look came over Blue Eagle's face. "I know. I heard everything," he said quietly.

Switch's lips pressed together and he averted his eyes. His father knew an unpowered henchman had him at his mercy due to his power issues. He had hoped he wouldn't.

Blue Eagle turned to Warren. "Are you okay, Your Honor?"

Warren nodded, still leaning against the wall with his hand over his heart. "I'm okay. Just a little shaken," he panted. He took a deep breath and smiled. "Not my first attempted kidnapping."

Everyone turned toward Poster Boy, who lay unconscious in a heap on the pavement.

A look of concern came over Warren's face. "Is....Is that young man....?"

"He's fine," said Blue Eagle, picking Poster Boy up and hoisting him over his shoulder. "I didn't hit him that hard. Just enough to knock him out. I will bring him to the police and they'll do the rest."

Switch found himself looking around as the adults were talking, Warren wondering what reason Poster Boy would have to do this and Blue Eagle promising to get to the bottom of it.

And then his eyes fell on the metal rectangle lying on the pavement only a few feet away from where Blue Eagle picked up Poster Boy.

He knelt down and flipped it over.

It was the car's license plate, shaken loose when Poster Boy was slammed into the trunk.

This was a lead to those two henchmen. Two henchmen that had just been working for Blizz Kid a few days ago to rob a research lab, and now were helping Poster Boy kidnap the mayor.

He glanced over at Blue Eagle and Warren. They were still talking about the situation and whether it was safe to continue the event. Neither of them noticed him.

It was obvious what he should do. And that was to immediately show Blue Eagle and Mayor Warren the license plate so it could be run and those two men could be brought to justice. It was to immediately tell them that there might be a connection between Poster Boy and Blizz Kid, possibly a villain team up.

"You're not going to have a solo career any time soon. At this rate, you'll only ever be a sidekick."

Instead, he quietly pulled his phone from his belt and took a picture, then picked up the license plate and shoved it in his belt right at the middle of his back. Hopefully his cape would keep anyone from seeing it.

This was his moment. Switch the Blue Eaglet was going to prove that he was more than just a sidekick.

He was going to get to the bottom of what was going on. And no one—especially his father—would ever be able to deny that he had what it took to be a solo superhero.

Chapter 8

"You've got Rosa with you?"

Jasper was walking down the last couple flights of his apartment building. The flip phone he used to talk to his wife was old and cheap, refurbished from the days before smartphones.

"Good to hear. I'll make sure I take her to school this week since I know you have an early shift."

He got to the ground floor and walked down the hall to the building exit. The pale beige walls and ceiling always reminded him of a rundown elementary school. Or the offices of a detention center. His footsteps echoed off the linoleum floors.

"Sorry, honey, I won't be home until late," he told his wife. "I got another job today that should hopefully be worth the next installment payment on our loan."

He pushed the door to the building open.

"I love you, too. Talk to you soon."

He closed the phone and moved to put it in his jacket.

"Nice! Is that a flip phone? How retro," came a young voice as a hand clasped his shoulder.

Jasper cried out as he whirled around to see Switch the Blue Eaglet standing before him. A thousand questions ran through his mind. How did he find him? Should he run? Could he possibly convince Switch he wasn't a criminal?

All Switch gave him in return was a flat stare. "Hang on," he said. "We need to talk."

Grasping Jasper under his arms, he floated into the air. He ignored Jasper's screaming as they flew to the rooftop of the ten story slum. They touched down on top of the building, and Jasper stumbled away as Switch released him.

Switch gave him another flat stare as he watched him hold his hand over his heart. "Oh, stop it. You're fine," he said as Jasper panted like he just finished a morning run.

Jasper looked around. There was no one else but the two of them. He decided to play the indignant civilian, hoping it would be enough to trick a teenager.

"Switch the Blue Eaglet?" he asked in still-not-quite-feigned shock. "Does Blue Eagle know you're wandering the Cellar District, grabbing random people off the street and disappearing them like that so-called hero Bloodpayne?"

Switch scoffed. "Please. I'm familiar with Bloodpayne. You should be thankful it was me who found you and not him. You've seen the news. You know what he does to people."

"W-why should I?" asked Jasper nervously. He looked around, half expecting Bloodpayne or one of the other superheroes from the murderous Dark Age of Heroes to show up. He was certain the superheroes all knew each other. "I'm a law-abiding citizen. I'm no criminal!"

"Jasper Clemens. Wife, Carla, and daughter, Rosa," said Switch, not moving his gaze away from Jasper. "You were the driver of the vehicle in Poster Boy's attempt to kidnap the mayor. And I remember now that you were also one of Blizz Kid's henchmen during the Herald City BioGenetics Research Lab attack."

Jasper swallowed hard. The kid had him dead to rights. "How did you find me?"

"From this," answered Switch, reaching behind his back and pulling out the license plate he had tucked in his back, hidden under his cape. He held it up and tapped on the numbers. "I think this belongs to you. Pro-tip: Don't use your personal vehicle as the getaway car for a kidnapping plot. It makes you really easy to track."

That was it. There was no getting out of this now. Jasper's shoulders slumped in defeat. "Is Blue Eagle gonna attack me if I try to run?" he asked meekly. "Because I ain't runnin'. I'm caught."

"I know you're not gonna run because you're *not* caught," corrected Switch. "I'm not arresting you."

Jasper blinked, but otherwise said nothing. The relief that should have flooded through him didn't come. All he felt was confusion.

After a few seconds of silence, Switch leaned forward and asked, "What was Blizz Kid trying to steal from that lab?"

There was a brief pause before Jasper shrugged half-heartedly. "I dunno. Just some gizmo the scientists were working on," he answered.

That was true. He didn't know. Henchmen didn't ask questions. They followed instructions.

"Fine. Let's talk about Poster Boy," said Switch. "Why did he try to kidnap the mayor?"

Another shrug. "I don't know what crazy plan that kid had. They don't tell us nothin'," said Jasper. "Plus, supervillains in this city have been kidnapping the mayor long before you were born."

Switch scratched his chin. "That's true. So let's do a more interesting one." He folded his arms. "That guy that tried to shoot me. He was also at the lab. Who is he?"

Jasper hesitated for a moment, dreading answering that question. He shook his head. "No way. I don't wanna rat on anyone," he finally answered. "Superhero interrogation or not, if everyone finds out you're a snitch, they take it out on your family if they can't take it out on you."

"I understand," said Switch softly. He sighed. "But I need answers. So here's one. In both encounters with that other guy, he touched people's necks in some *weird* way."

"He touched their necks?"

"Yeah. Like...." Switch turned and tilted his head forward so Jasper could see him imitating the motion, pinching the back of his own neck slightly with his thumb and index finger. "Is there anything going on with that?"

"I dunno. Sorry, I don't know what you're talking about," lied Jasper. He distinctly remembered Clay touching the back of Blizz Kid's neck that way, though nothing actually happened with that. He chalked it up at the time to Clay being *Clay*. He loved making people feel uneasy.

Switch didn't say anything. Instead, he looked the low level criminal up and down, as if trying to determine whether or not he believed Jasper's story.

After a moment, it appeared he did.

"Twice in as many times seeing you, I saw you do the right thing," he said finally. " You didn't have to unload that gun, but you did. And at the lab, you were going to surrender peacefully. I remember. And

I think you'll do the right thing again. Maybe you have to work up the nerve, or maybe you have to work out some arrangements for what happens when you do, but I don't think you're really a bad guy. And I think I can count on you to do the right thing when the time comes."

He reached into his belt and pulled out a piece of paper, handing it to Jasper.

"What is this?" asked Jasper.

"My phone number. In case you have any more information or insight into future supervillain attacks. Don't call for Blue Eagle. This ain't the Eagle Eye Tip Line. This is just me."

"The Eagle Eye Tip Line? Is that a real thing?

"No." Switch thought for a moment. "That would be pretty cool though."

"Why don't you want me to speak to Blue Eagle?"

Again, Switch hesitated before answering. "Blue Eagle is a busy man. He's out there looking for big fish to fry. I deal with the small fry in the meantime."

That answer didn't quite convince Jasper, but he wasn't about to argue considering the teen superhero was well within his rights to beat him up and drag him to jail.

Switch turned and started to climb onto the roof's ledge. "Well, I'm done here," he announced. With one foot on the ledge, he turned slightly back. "But I hope you make use of that number, if there's a reason to."

"Aren't you at least gonna give me a lift back down?"

"Nope. You can walk and use that time to think about things."

They stood there in silence, Switch with one leg on the ledge preparing to fly away.

"Are *you* going back down?" Jasper finally asked.

"In a minute. I'm just waiting for my cooldown to end."

There was another beat before Jasper spoke again.

"That kinda takes away from the moment."

"It kinda does."

Chapter 9

A dozen small time, two-bit henchmen, including Jasper, were led by Clay out of the mineshaft hallway and into what seemed to be an untended garden. Most of the room had loose soil instead of a solid floor. Rows of incandescent lights did, at best, a serviceable job of keeping the area lit.

Jasper shivered. The air was heavy with danger. Someone was going to suffer and die in this room. He could feel it.

He just hoped it wasn't him.

"Nice place," said one of the thugs.

"I figured the lady would tend to her garden a little better," said another.

Clay ignored them. "Stay there," he ordered. To seemingly no one in particular, he turned and announced, "I've brought the hired help."

A door on the opposite end of the room, past the soil, opened. In walked Blizz Kid.

Followed by Poster Boy.

Confused murmurs echoed from the henchmen.

"Poster Boy? Ain't he supposed to be locked up in the Cinder Block? I thought he got arrested," said one thug.

"I heard Blue Eagle took him down again. What gives?" chimed in another.

Jasper glanced toward Clay, who didn't return his look. The more dangerous crook had a hard expression that was somewhere between apathy and hostility, like he was waiting for one of the others to start a fight with him. He wondered what Clay knew about Poster Boy's miraculous appearance.

The supervillains said nothing as they stood aside for another person that entered.

Jasper gasped in shock as Mayor Michael Warren strode into the garden and stood on the dirt next to the villains.

"Ain't that the mayor!?" asked another thug quite loudly.

Three more people walked in. Two of them, Jasper didn't recognize. He was a bookish man in a suit that seemed slightly too big, and the other was a heavyset man with calloused hands and business casual clothing.

But then out came the woman that Clay had taken hostage at the research lab over a week ago. This time, she didn't appear to be under duress, nor did she seem affected by being in the same room with Clay. She just stood with a muted expression on her face next to the other two men. They all had similar expressions of disinterest.

"Who the heck are these suits?" asked one of the henchmen with confusion and disdain.

"They are my subjects."

Everyone but Clay jumped at the sound of the regal female voice behind them. They whirled around to see a vibrant jungle where nothing but dirt lay just moments ago. Lush vegetation covered a quarter of the room, blocking the tunnel that led them down here. Thick leaves hung from trees that reached all the way up to the ceiling.

The henchmen looked at each other uneasily as the bushes and grass began to quiver, as if something were slowly coming towards them.

Queen Venus stepped majestically from the seven foot tall flowers at the center of the greenery. The henchmen all nervously parted so she could pass wordlessly between them. She did not so much as acknowledge their existence.

She stood next to the mayor. Turning toward the henchmen, she gestured toward the lineup of unknowns.

"Michael Warren. Mayor of Herald City," she introduced. She waved a hand toward each of them in the order they came in. "Next is Marcel Kui, City Parks Commissioner. Herald City BioGenetic Research Lab Project Lead Doctor Paige Roberts. And lastly, Tony Bruscetti, CEO of Superheroic Construction Enterprises Inc."

She nodded toward the villains. "And of course you're familiar with Poster Boy and Blizz Kid, two of Herald City's younger supervillains. Specifically, Blue Eagle's villains."

"Uh, question," came the voice of one of the henchmen, half-heartedly raising his hand. "Clay and

Jasper said Blue Eagle took Poster Boy down. So how's he here?"

"Easy. I *made* friends in high places," responded Queen Venus pointedly.

The henchmen murmured amongst themselves in confusion. Jasper, as always, kept quiet. There was something about the way she said those words that made the hairs on the back of his neck stand up.

"Allow me to explain," she began. "I have the power to create and control plants. They can come from my body—"

A pair of thick vines erupted from her shoulder blades. Their tips turned toward the henchmen, splitting open like mouths. Even the hardened criminals cried out in fear at the high pitched wail the vines made.

"—or they can come out of anywhere I please."

A pair of sunflowers as high as her chest burst out of the dirt in front of her. Their "faces" whirled toward the henchmen, shaking as if laughing at them. The screechy giggle sound they emitted made Jasper think they *were* laughing at them.

He suddenly desperately wanted to be at home with his wife and daughter.

"Along with that are the toxins that run through my body in place of blood," she continued. The vines and flowers retracted like a tape measure back into its holder. "They can create acidic liquids or gas that can paralyze you or temporarily take away superpowers, and give me strength comparable to Blue Eagle. But my plants, when I exert my will on them, are mentally controlled by me. Behold!"

Everyone took a step back as the dirt in front of them began to quiver and part. A pair of creatures reached out and pulled themselves out of the ground. They were humanoid, about six feet tall, and faceless messes of vines and leaves. The grotesque parodies of men stood facing the nervous crooks.

"I can make my plant men do anything. I can make them hostile...."

The plant monsters grabbed the two nearest thugs by their shirts. One of them let out a high pitched feminine shriek.

"....or I can make them do a little dance."

The monsters released the men and stepped back. They suddenly broke out into an Irish jig, dancing enthusiastically to music that no one could hear.

"Or I can make them rush into certain freezing death."

The plant monsters turned on their heels and rushed toward Blizz Kid. He casually held out a palm, and a blast of arctic air enveloped one, freezing it in place. He punched the second one in the gut, his fist tearing into its wet and pulpy flesh. Its insides began to freeze, ice expanding all over its body until it stopped moving. In one final display of his power, he formed an ice sword in one hand and sliced both creatures in half at the waist.

Jasper gulped. He didn't even notice himself instinctively placing his hand protectively over one hip.

As Blizz Kid's blade melted from his hand, Queen Venus turned to the henchmen and explained, "Those creatures were a part of me. They did what they did because I willed them to."

After a beat, she seemed to narrow her masked eyes on each one of them.

"So is Blizz Kid."

The room was so quiet that the sound of small pieces of dirt falling from the leaves behind them felt as loud as dishes breaking in a restaurant. No one dared to breathe. What did she mean by that?

She dropped her menacing stare and went back to her lecture-like monologue. "In the past, I've been too concerned about *conquering* and *ruling* the people of Herald City. But why do all that when you can just make the people an extension of yourself?" she explained. "Through my natural knowledge of plants, I was able to develop my *Planticite*, a tiny plant that, when pressed against the back of someone's neck, burrows inside and lives inside like a parasite. Living inside a person's nervous system, it allows me to 'mindjack' people, as I like to call it, and control them as part of my plants."

"Recently, I've been hard at work getting certain people in positions of power mindjacked," she continued. She circled around Clay, keeping her eyes on him as she still addressed the group. "And thanks to Mr. Clayton, formerly a local gang member before I got my tendrils on him—figuratively speaking, of course—I now have the individuals you see before you. As well as others carrying out tasks elsewhere."

Clay had a look of satisfaction on his face as she praised him. Jasper wondered if their relationship was more than just professional, but stifled the thought. He didn't even know who—or *what*—was behind that mask.

"That must be how Poster Boy got free," blurted out the thug standing next to Jasper.

Queen Venus turned to him. "That is correct," she confirmed after a pause. "Poster Boy was released by a high ranking official because I willed him to be released by a high ranking official."

She looked around the room and clasped her hands. "I imagine you're all wondering, of course, what my plan is. What my endgame is," she said, a sudden delightful spark in her voice. "I think I'll allow my *plants* to explain their role."

"Blizz Kid and I were just distractions," said Poster Boy, stepping forward. "I was never intended to successfully kidnap the mayor. It was all a ruse to implant someone else at that event with a Planticite, and the ruse was a success. The mayor was already mindjacked weeks ago. Now, no one will think of the kidnapping attempt as anything more than that."

He glanced at Blizz Kid and smirked. "Blizz Kid wasn't mindjacked when he attacked the lab, by the way. He just failed his mission. but that was okay because mindjacking Doctor Roberts was the primary objective. He didn't know that at the time.

"What are you implying!?" demanded Blizz Kid. "I can kill you right now in an instant!"

"You can kill me. Can you kill *all* of me?"

"I don't see your picture up anywhere."

"If you want something to lovingly gaze at, I can always—"

"Boys, settle down," interrupted Queen Venus, a hint of playful amusement in her voice.

Slowly, the teen villains turned to her, their eyes dull and glassy. "Yes, Your Grace," they said in a monotone unison.

Doctor Paige Roberts from the Herald City BioGenetics Research Lab stepped forward. "Unfortunately, the process of mindjacking people was too slow, requiring someone to physically implant the Planticite into the back of someone's neck," she explained. "And while controlling the people in power is nice, Queen Venus isn't into politicking. The goal is to have full control over *everyone*. But how will she achieve that? Through my Photosynthesis Enhancer, which is what Blizz Kid was sent to steal from the BioGenetics Lab. It's a device of my own design that enhances a plant's ability to process sunlight and turn it into energy by a hundredfold."

She shrugged. "I initially conceived of it as a way to address deforestation and climate change, but this is good too," she added. "With some additional materials and modifications, it can be used to create a Planticite factory and distribution center!"

"It will be located at Liberty Park. Doctor Roberts has already sent the device there after Blizz Kid's initial robbery attempt," chimed in Warren, taking over the conversation.

"Which, remember, Blizz Kid wasn't mindjacked for," reminded Poster Boy with a smug grin on his face. "He didn't know he was just a distraction. He failed that 100% on his own."

"Yes, which was the desired outcome. With the machine being delivered by its creator rather than stolen, we avoid suspicion and an active search by law enforcement for the device," clarified Warren over the sound of a growl from the ice villain. "Now, you've heard of the Liberty Park Opportunity Project, the office building construction project at Liberty Park? That's specifically our cover for this factory. Due to the unpopularity of having a large construction project at Liberty Park, the city would never approve this. But after Clay here infected myself and the others here with Planticite, we're of one mind. We have all the people we need to force this project through."

"I carried out Mayor Warren's orders to get a foundation built at Liberty Park, calling in favors and greasing palms even as all the legislators and bureaucrats demanded that the project be completely terminated," said Parks Commissioner Kui, stepping forward as he continued the explanation. "In the end—and with the help of a Planticite—we awarded the contract to Superheroic Construction Enterprises Inc."

"Queen Venus has the ability to grow her plants to incredible sizes, but for what she wanted to build, a professionally made foundation was necessary," explained Tony Bruscetti, the CEO, in a thick New York accent. "As the largest general contractor in Herald City, my company was the perfect one to carry out Queen Venus' will and create the foundation she needs to build it."

"And with the Photosynthesis Enhancer and a foundation at Liberty Park ready, I shall give life to my greatest creation. My *Treescraper*!" declared Queen Venus, spreading her arms theatrically. "Whereas humanity builds their giant towers out of iron and steel and concrete, I will use the Photosynthesis Enhancer, some extra materials, and my powers to create a skyscraper of wood and leaves and pulp! One of true power and connected to nature that towers over the city skyline!"

With a throaty chuckle, she continued, "And from this Treescraper, the Photosynthesis Enhancer will be able to instantly produce Planticites en masse and transport them through sunlight into whatever targets I choose. And my targets will be everyone in Herald City!" She began to cackle madly. "And once I have control over the city, the whole *world* will come next!"

Over the sound of her evil laughter came the cheers of one thug, then another, and another. Men who had little in life and nothing to lose pumped their fists into the air and cheered for a chance at power and control. Dominance.

Jasper thought he was going to be sick.

Chapter 10

Switch stood there on the rooftop, stunned by what Jasper just told him.

"So.... So Queen Venus was behind both the BioGenetics Lab attack and the attempt to kidnap the mayor," he repeated back to Jasper. "And both were distractions to keep everyone from noticing what she was doing."

"That's right," said Jasper, leaning against the ledge.

"And her plan is to use this Photosynthesis Enhancer thingy to build a giant skyscraper tree that will mass produce those Planticite things--the parasites that she's been using to turn people like the mayor over to her side without anyone knowing~and put them inside everyone in Herald City so that she will control them like her plants," Switch continued to summarize.

"Everyone in the whole *world*," corrected Jasper.

Switch nodded. "That's pretty standard supervillain aspirations, and Queen Venus isn't the type to stop at just the whole city. But this scheme?"

He thought for a moment, gazing out over the city as he rested his elbows on the ledge. A light afternoon breeze blew towards him, causing his cape to flap slightly.

"Queen Venus isn't *the* top villain in Herald City—that title tends to go to the Defending Champions' main villain—but she *is* the archenemy of Blue Eagle and has been since a little after I started three years ago," he explained to Jasper. "She's risen the ranks faster than any other supervillain and is one of the most dangerous ever. We've thwarted her plans so many times, but we could never actually catch her. Blue Eagle and I, I mean."

"I know. She's known to be bad news."

"She's done some pretty crazy stuff over the years and nearly destroyed the city multiple times," he continued. "But this? The advantage she has right now? Controlling the whole government as if they were her plants? Being so close to controlling *everyone?*"

With a sigh, he turned to Jasper.

"I wanted to get to the bottom of this on my own, but now that it's Queen Venus we're dealing with? I have to get Blue Eagle involved."

Jasper raised an eyebrow. "So Blue Eagle *isn't* already?"

Switch shot him a surprised look, then realized what he just blurted out. "I wanted to go solo on this one. Do things my way. Have you feed me intel rather than just put another crook in jail," he muttered, his shoulders slumped in defeat.

"Then how are you gonna get the big man in on this without telling him where you got this information from?" pressed Jasper. "I know he's big on being tough on crime and all that. I can't afford to go to jail. Not when my family needs me."

Switch thought for another moment, then shook his head. "I dunno, but I'll think of something. I'm not gonna throw you under the bus," he answered.

Jasper sighed and nodded. It was the best answer he could possibly get at the moment.

"Now, Blue Eagle and I will have to check out the Liberty Park construction site if we're gonna stop Queen Venus," considered Switch, his mind already switching gears toward how to defeat his nemesis. "Unless....you wouldn't happen to know where her current lair is, would you?"

"No, sorry. We were blindfolded when we were brought in and out."

"Liberty Park it is, then."

There was a moment of silence before Jasper tapped the ledge and pushed away. "Well, good luck, kid. I hope it all works out, but I ain't stayin' in Herald long enough to see," he said dismissively, starting toward the rooftop entrance.

"What do you mean? I need you to continue feeding me information from the inside," said Switch as he whirled around.

It was Jasper's turn to turn around. "Oh no, I'm done. I'm taking a big enough risk as is talking to you," he said, holding his hands up. "Supervillains don't treat henchmen very well. If Queen Venus ever finds out about this conversation, I'm a dead man."

"So that's it? With what's at stake, your plan is to just up and leave?" the teenage sidekick shot back.

"Yeah, actually! Frankly, I'm done with this whole gig. I desperately need money, but getting money from this job is gonna put me in more danger than not getting it at all. Just *being* in this rotten city is dangerous. So I'm out."

"What are you talking about? You're not getting out of this. Not after what you did."

Confusion washed over Jasper's face. "What do you mean 'after what I did'?" he asked.

"You were a henchman in Blizz Kid's lab heist, where you were armed and a lot of innocents almost got killed," reminded Switch. "You were the getaway driver in an attempted kidnapping of the mayor when your buddy, Clay, almost killed me!"

Sweat formed on Jasper's brow. "Now, now wait a minute! I didn't hurt nobody," he argued nervously. "I mean, I saved your life!"

"I appreciate that, which is why you're not in jail right now. But you're still a criminal. You still chose to be a supervillain henchman. Did you think it was a job you could just quit?"

"I never chose to be a criminal," said Jasper quietly, his expression darkening.

"What do you mean?" asked Switch, echoes of frustration still in his voice. "Were you kidnapped, or threatened into joining her operation?"

For a moment, nothing was said. Jasper's gaze was off in the distance, toward the tops of nearby buildings in the dirty Cellar District. He shuffled over to the rooftop ledge, resting his elbows on the chest-high cement as he looked over the city.

"I wasn't kidnapped or anything. But no, I didn't choose this life," he finally said. He paused, then turned his head toward Switch. "Tell me, Switch. You ever talk to the henchmen you and your dad put away?"

"What? Do we—Yeah, of course I have," lied Switch. The question caught him by surprise. Henchmen were usually just faceless goons to him. Interchangeable punching bags he had to get through to fight the actual supervillain.

He felt a sudden twinge of shame.

"A lot of these guys don't want to be caught up in all this and are trying to get out," continued Jasper, ignoring Switch's insincerity. "Not Clay, of course. But guys like me. And my story is particularly bad."

"Yeah? What happened?" asked Switch, leaning against the ledge next to him.

"On the surface, it doesn't seem *that* bad. There's no bad choice I made that came back to haunt me," began Jasper. He sighed heavily. "It's that there never *was* a choice in my life. In anything. My parents were immigrants. They came here and got stuck living in the worst neighborhoods with nothing to their name, and they couldn't afford schooling for their kids. They scraped up money to start a business, but that fell to racketeering operations by the mob that the cops looked the other way on. I had to drop outta high school and work to keep food on the table when my old man turned to crime to keep us afloat and ended up in the state penn for twenty."

"I'm sorry to hear that."

"I got older, got married, had a daughter, and the cycle continued," Jasper continued his tale. "No one would hire me and I couldn't save any money. The price of everything just kept goin' up and up and up. We turned to payday loans to make ends meet, and then loan sharks. I got into crime to pay all the debts and bills that wouldn't stop piling up, and now I am where I am now."

He let out a heavy sigh. "You just don't understand that life," he said.

"I do," said Switch. "I know all about it."

"Really? Have you lived that life? Have you experienced poverty?" challenged Jasper, turning to the boy. "You ever have to move because you couldn't afford to stay in a place? You ever not sure when you would get your next meal?"

Switch's face grew red. "No," he answered, averting his eyes. "We live in Greengrove. Blue Eagle sells insurance and occasionally does endorsements on the side."

"Greengrove. That's an upper middle class neighborhood," noted Jasper. "You have things pretty good, Switch. You're a lucky kid who can choose to be a superhero or can choose to do something else."

"I've read a lot lately," offered Switch hastily. "About poverty and criminal reform and everything."

"That's nice, but this ain't some academic paper. I'm a real person with real problems. I have a family to feed with no money to do so."

"So what *are* you going to do for money then?"

"Dunno. I'm thinkin' me and the missus will take our daughter and leave town with a go-bag and the clothes on our backs. That is," Jasper shot Switch a glance, "if you'll let me."

Again, Switch thought for a moment. He knew what he was *supposed* to do, what Blue Eagle would do. And that was to take the criminal standing next to him to the police so he could be put in prison where he belonged. Jasper already took direct part in kidnapping and hostage taking. Who knew what other crimes were under his belt?

And even casting that aside, he knew what was the most prudent thing to do. That was to keep this valuable source of intel for as long as possible. Jasper could get him information, or be used to feed fake information to Queen Venus in order to set her up. What did it matter if he didn't want to keep putting himself in danger? Crooks didn't get choices. They got jail time.

"You have my number," murmured Switch, not meeting Jasper's gaze. He activated his flight. "Please reach out to me if you change your mind," he added, flying away. As he did, he wondered if it was enlightened defiance or a fear of making the tough choices that made him let this criminal go scot free.

For a while, Jasper didn't move. He felt a sense of wrongness on the pit of his stomach. Getting his family out of Herald City was his first priority, and deciding to finally leave—even if they had to leave everything they owned behind and enter a new state blind—was the right choice.

Choice.

It felt like the first choice he ever made in his life. The first *real* one, one with a real impact on his future. He *knew* he was making the right one.

But he couldn't shake the feeling he made the wrong one.

He took one last look at the rooftops. The area that he lived in was one of the most crime-infested parts of Herald City. Trash and grime were everywhere, and the streets felt like they were always hiding something dangerous at night.

But it wasn't night. It was late morning. And right now....

"It's actually a pretty view this time o' day," he remarked to no one in particular before heading for the rooftop entrance.

He took one step inside before passing out from the chloroform rag someone pressed against his face.

Chapter 11

The sudden bright light stung Jasper's eyes as they fluttered open. He brought a hand up to block the stinging light, only to find he couldn't actually raise it. He felt a snap of confusion as he realized he couldn't move his arms or legs at all.

Confusion turned to panic when he realized his arms and legs were duct taped to a chair.

He frantically looked around, gasping for air as if he had just finished running a marathon. There wasn't much to see. It was a dark room with one bright light bulb hanging directly overhead.

"Wha—Where am—wha—?" he sputtered.

"Wakey, wakey, Mister Clemens," sang a voice behind him.

Jasper swore loudly as Mickey, the Charlemagne Family loan shark, stepped into view. His burly bodyguard was with him.

"Now, now, Mister Clemens. Settle down. I just brought you here to talk finance," said Mickey as another muscular man—a bald African-American man in a tight yellow T-shirt—stepped into Jasper's view.

"What are you talking about!? I paid! I paid that installment on my loan!" cried Jasper.

"You did," said Mickey. "But the mob needs money for its own reasons and so the deadline to pay back your debts in full has been moved up to *now*."

Jasper's jaw dropped as he looked back and forth between the two large enforcers—the "debt collectors". He struggled mightily in his chair. He didn't have money on him to pay them back.

Which meant they were either going to kill him, or injure him so severely he'd wish he were dead.

Mickey chuckled seeing him struggle. "Relax. I know you don't have the cash *on* you," he assured in a way that was more intimidating than reassuring. "I'm giving you a chance to come up with the cash now. We're gonna go with you to your house or to the

ATM or wherever else and you're gonna get whatever money you can to pay off your loan, and whatever balance remains, well...."

He gestured to the two enforcers. The black man pounded his palm with his fists.

"....my associates will collect the rest."

"But-but....I don't have the money to pay it all off! I need more time!" pleaded Jasper.

"There is no time. If you don't have the money now, well, I guess we can work off some of your debt right away. Then we can go and you can get us the rest."

Mickey stepped back as the two enforcers approached Jasper.

"*Three days!*" shouted Jasper in a panic. "Mickey, please! I work for Queen Venus! Just gimme three days!"

"Stop!" ordered Mickey.

The two massive enforcers stopped. They stepped aside as he approached the terrified captive. He looked Jasper up and down, as if determining whether or not to believe him.

"Go on," he pressed.

Jasper's widened eyes couldn't help but glance at the hungry enforcers. "I'm a Queen Venus henchman, and there's a big operation going down. Big job, big operation. Her biggest one yet," he rambled quickly. "I can't tell you about it, but it pays big."

"Queen Venus ain't known for using henchmen," noted Mickey, doubt in his voice. "She makes those creepy plants that look like humans."

One of the goons shuddered.

"It's a really big job. A long term operation," elaborated Jasper frantically. "But there's a smaller job that's needed very soon and I'll get money from that! Please, just three days and you'll have your money in full! I swear it."

The loan shark mulled it over for a moment. He pointed to the second man and then to Jasper.

"Mickey? Mickey, please, you'll get your money. I swear it," repeated Jasper.

He began to struggle as the enforcer approached him, a sinister smile on his face.

"Mickey, please, just three days! You'll get your money!" pleaded Jasper, frantically fighting his restraints as the huge goon clasped his shoulders, keeping him in place.

The loan shark approached Jasper, taking a switchblade out of his pocket. Jasper let out a cry as the blade flicked open. "Please! You'll get your money, I swear it!"

With a cruel glint in his eye, Mickey leaned forward so they were eye to eye.

"You've got three days, Clemens. Three days to pay back the agreed upon $5,000, plus late fees. And if you don't get the money in that time...." Mickey held the blade to Jasper's face for a second, then shook his head and pulled it back. "It will be Carla tied to that chair."

"You'll get your money," assured Jasper, hanging his head. Quietly, broken and defeated, he repeated, "You'll get your money."

"Good to hear," said Mickey, taking a couple steps back. He closed the switchblade and put it back in his pocket. "Thank you for your business. Our relationship has been good for the Charlemagne Family. As a token of my appreciation, my men will show you out."

Before he could say anything, Jasper fell unconscious again from the chloroform rag shoved in his face.

Chapter 12

Beams of frost covered the fleeing civilians, freezing them in place. Grinning men with high tech freeze guns ran up to their victims, who protested and pleaded to be unfrozen as they were robbed blind. The thieves took men's wallets and women's jewelry.

One particularly cruel criminal reached into a stroller and stole the lollipop from the crying baby within.

The sound of sirens blared in the distance. Three police cars turned the corner, speeding toward the group of criminals causing an icy havoc through the city streets. Their charge was stopped short by the sudden iceberg that formed from the pavement directly below them. The cars launched ten feet into the air and landed upside down.

Blizz Kid stood in front of the half dozen ice-gun wielding henchmen, his hand still outstretched toward the cop cars he destroyed.

"Uh uh! No interference from the boys in blue," he said as the cops crawled from their patrol cars. He grinned. "Though I am waiting for a pair that is known to wear the color."

On the other side of town, in a busy commercial district, advertisement posters were coming to life!

Clones of Poster Boy leapt out of each image, eliciting screams of terror from shoppers, employees, and passersby alike. The supervillain avatars pulled handguns from their belts and held up whoever was closest.

Casually strolling though the streets, past mugging after mugging, was the real Poster Boy. A satisfied grin spread across his face. He felt the thrill of every exercise of power over the helpless people around him.

"The Father-Son Duo have no idea what's about to hit them," he declared with gleeful anticipation.

A black van sat parked on the street just around the corner. A man wearing a black turtleneck and pants ran towards it and entered into the back.

"Poster Boy's doing his thing and he's got a whole crowd held up," he reported to the others as he settled into one of the seats.

"Pretty impressive," said another sitting next to him. "I guess that's why the tights-wearers are the supervillains and we're the small timers nobody cares about."

In the front passenger seat, Clay patted his illegal automatic machine gun. "Don't worry about fame. Because the pay we're gonna get will be outta this world," he assured them. He turned to face them. "Now lock and load, gents! Time to get to work!"

The thugs let out a cheer, loading their weapons.

Amongst the cheering criminals, in the front seat, was Jasper. He pumped a fist in the air, consciously keeping a look of excitement on his face. But as he looked away, he couldn't help the expression and feeling of shame that threatened to overtake him.

It hurt him to be here doing this.

But he didn't have a choice.

Chapter 13

High above the Herald City skyline flew the Father-Son Duo of Blue Eagle and Switch the Blue Eaglet.

It was not a particularly dignified affair. That was why they usually flew as high up as possible. They wanted to avoid the public eye as much as they could.

Due to his power limitations, Switch couldn't fly long distances without the risk of falling out of the sky. Using his superspeed was also impractical. It would shut off before he could get to where they needed to go. Plus, their different modes of travel would mean they couldn't go to whatever dangerous place they were going to together and work out a plan.

So instead, Blue Eagle held Switch by his waist and carried him through the skies.

Undignified, and embarrassing at first. But they were used to it.

That wasn't what was on either superhero's mind at the moment, however. Instead, it was a seemingly strange suggestion from Switch.

"Why are you so insistent on checking out the Liberty Park construction site?" asked Blue Eagle.

"There's just something suspicious about it," replied Switch, his mind nervously trying to remember the brilliant excuse that seemed not so brilliant right now. "I mean....it's really unpopular, and it's out of character for Mayor Warren to try to have some big industrialization project in the middle of a nature section of the city's biggest public park."

"I'm glad you're concerned about public corruption," said Blue Eagle in a way that sounded like he wasn't glad, "but what does that have to do with Blizz Kid freezing people solid in Downtown and Poster Boy robbing people in Highland Heights?"

"Well, uh, do you think it's weird at all that two of *our* villains are pulling big public attacks at the same time, just after they individually had their own smaller ones?"

"I've considered that, and we can figure out later if the two are working together on something bigger. But right now the top priority is to stop the attacks they're currently doing. And Liberty Park has nothing to do with any of that."

"But what if it does?" blurted Switch. He thought quickly. "What if there's something bigger going on, bigger even than two supervillains working together, and it's coming from a larger plot involving corruption and forcing an unpopular and destructive construction project through? One whose completion could have devastating consequences for the city!"

Blue Eagle raised an eyebrow, casting a confused look at his son. "Switch, what on *Earth* are you talking about?"

Switch's face turned beet red. He felt so stupid. And helpless. Queen Venus was working toward her evil goals in Liberty Park as they spoke, and there was no way to convince his father to check it out without compromising Jasper's role in everything.

And if Blue Eagle knew he was protecting a criminal, he'd be in more trouble than he has ever been in his life.

He knew they had to stop Poster Boy and Blizz Kid. They were Blue Eagle and Switch's enemies, and therefore their responsibility. That's how it worked in Herald City; superheroes stopped the supervillains in their own Rogues Gallery. And dealing with Queen Venus—their own archnemesis—could probably wait until after Blizz Kid and Poster Boy were subdued.

But he couldn't shake the feeling that this simultaneous attack was happening for a reason. That Queen Venus was closer to achieving her goals than he thought.

"Sorry. Never mind," he finally mumbled, wishing he hadn't said anything.

Blue Eagle chuckled. "Do you know anything I don't?"

"No," sighed Switch as people below watched them fly off into the distance. "Just a stupid feeling."

Chapter 14

A school bus drove through Downtown Herald City, its seats filled with the students it just picked up from the city's top public elementary school minutes ago. The driver swerved suddenly as a light blue beam hit the cars ahead of him, freezing them solid. The chatter and laughter of children turned to high pitched shrieks and screams as the bus felt like it was about to tip over.

The kids pressed against the windows to see what was happening outside. Whimpers of fear sounded throughout the bus at the sight of three men in heavy snow coats and freeze ray guns approaching them. Beams of blue light danced over the muzzles of the criminals' weapons, and menacing grins covered their faces.

Behind them was Blizz Kid. Even through his ski goggles, it was clear that there was no mercy in his eyes.

"It's going to be okay. It'll be okay," assured the attendant on the school bus as she saw some of the kids start to cry. "Everyone, put on your coats and zip up tight. It's going to get a little cold, but your coats should keep you warm!"

Blizz Kid sneered as he looked at the terrified young faces in the windows. "Freeze the bus," he ordered his men.

The children screamed in fear, holding each other in anticipation as the henchmen aimed their weapons at the bus. They cried out again as the beams went under the bus and the ground moved further and further away from them.

Then they cheered.

Blue Eagle had arrived just in time. He floated a dozen feet over the pavement, holding the bus over his head with two hands.

He set the bus down facing the direction it had come from and floated to the driver's window. "Get as far away from here as you can."

"You got it, Blue Eagle," acknowledged the driver, stepping on the bus and driving away.

The children waved at the superhero as they went by, happy to be safe from the bad guys. He smiled at them; a soft, genuine smile. He always liked that.

His smile turned to a dark glare as he turned towards the criminals who tried to harm them.

"If there's one thing I don't like," he growled, floating to the ground and striding purposefully toward the villain and his minions, "it's when lowlife thugs target children."

One of the henchmen gave a sickening smirk. "Speaking of children, where's that kid sidekick of yours?" he asked, patting his freeze gun. "I wanna put a couple of birds on ice."

A blue and white blur of speed rushed past him from behind, ripping his weapon from his hand and throwing it back at his face before he even had a chance to cry out. Switch skidded to a stop, his cape whipping around theatrically just as the unconscious thug hit the floor.

"Switch the Blue Eagle, at your service," he broadcasted with a grin on his face. "Oh, buddy—well, you can't hear me, but I'll say it for your friends' benefit—if you're gonna call me a child as an insult, don't work for a teenage supervillain."

"I see you didn't like that guy," noted Blizz Kid. "Well, let me bring over some more playmates for you and maybe you'll click better with them."

"'Playmates'? Not you, too. Dude, we're the *same age*," muttered Switch as Blizz Kid let out a loud whistle.

At the sound, six more henchmen—all armed with freeze ray guns of their own—rushed from the other streets and alleys to Blizz Kid's side. The supervillain was now protected by eight ice-wielding henchmen.

"Double pay for anyone who brings me an ice statue of Switch the Blue Eaglet," announced the ice-powered villain. "And *triple pay* for anyone who brings me an ice statue of Blue Eagle!"

"It looks like we're in high demand as collectors' items," quipped Switch, readying himself for battle.

"Unfortunately, the people frozen in those cars are apparently just throwaways," said Blue Eagle, noticing the people trapped just past the villains in their frozen cars, shivering from the cold and failing to break through the ice to freedom. "Switch, you deal with the henchmen and rescue those people. *I'll* deal with Blizz Kid."

The villain's eyes widened with gleeful anticipation. "Oh, you're gonna *deal* with me?"

He raised his arm, and an aura of frost and mist flowed from his body and surrounded him. Vapor turned to water and then to ice, attaching to his body. Faster than chemistry and physics would normally allow, more and more ice clumped and smoothed out over his arms, legs, and chest. Thick gauntlets of ice covered his hands, and boots formed on his feet.

When it was done and the aura faded into the air as fine mist, he was clad from head to toe in armor made of thick ice. Only his face remained uncovered.

"Alright, *deal*," he challenged, locking eyes with Blue Eagle.

Chapter 15

A mighty fist slammed into a thick armor made of ice. Another punch connected against the armored ribs. A third hit the sternum.

Blue Eagle's powerful blows sent the armored Blizz Kid stumbling back. Ice chips scattered over the pavement. Cracks formed in the armor where the superhero's fists made contact.

Those cracks resealed themselves in seconds. The armor was once again intact.

Blizz Kid caught the momentary look of confusion on his opponent's face. "I'm wearing ice armor and I have ice powers," he said with a cocky grin. "Of course my armor can repair itself."

"Annoying, but no problem," huffed Blue Eagle. "That just means I'll have to *hit you harder!*"

He pushed off one foot, rocketing toward Blizz Kid like a missile. He reared back his fist, ready to deliver a thunderous right hook.

Blizz Kid twisted his body as the superhero flew toward him. With uncharacteristic strength, he backhanded Blue Eagle across the face, sending him careening through the glass display window of a nearby cafe.

"Surprised by that? You're not the only one that can throw a punch!" laughed the villain. "I can also control the mass and the density of my armor as I'm wearing it. More or less water in there, the harder I can hit or the faster I can move." He looked at his hands as he made a fist. "It's a bit heavy in the instant I want a hard hit, I'll admit, and I wish I had your strength to wield it more freely. But I think this trick will do for now."

Blue Eagle emerged from the cafe, eyeing Blizz Kid menacingly as he wiped some dust, debris, and a spot of heavy cream from his costume.

"*For now,*" he growled, his eyes glowing red.

"Missed!" quipped Switch as he dodged an ice beam.

Another blast came toward him, and again he was suddenly not there. A blur of blue and white jumped from one side of the street to another.

"Missed again!" he jeered as another ice beam missed its mark, freezing the mailbox behind him. "Ooh, destroying federal property? That's a no-no."

"Stand still, you obnoxious little brat!" yelled one of the six crooks in snow jackets firing their freeze guns at him.

"Come on, I'm doing the next best thing," taunted the teen, effortlessly dodging another blast. "As far as hitting a speedster goes, this is as easy as it gets. I can only move at about 100 miles per hour. With no acceleration, of course. There are guys out there that can outrun light!"

He seemed to instantly disappear as another blast of ice was fired at him. The sentient speed blur moved across the street, picking up a brick as he did so. Rushing toward a car with a freezing family trapped in it, he hurled the brick at the driver side door, shattering the door handle and locking mechanism.

"It's broken! Kick your way out!" shouted Switch, gesturing at them to break the door open.

The man in the driver's seat turned and kicked at the door, breaking it open. He scrambled out and turned to pull his wife and crying children to safety.

"Hey! How did they break out!?" cried a henchman, not having seen the superhero's fast moves.

"Ignore them! Focus on Switch!" ordered another.

"Hang on!" warned Switch, grabbing the two small children under his arm and rushing them at superspeed around the corner to the next block. He came back, scooped the startled woman up in his arms, and brought her to the same place.

He got back in time to see the driver running in that direction and was far enough away from the henchmen that they would target Switch instead.

Only one car was left with people inside. Two girls trapped and trying to force their car doors open with their feet, the ice too cold to touch with their bare hands.

He grabbed the loose brick. He didn't have much time left before his speed failed him.

The henchmen took aim at him.

"Freeze this little ba—" shouted one of them, the rest of his sentence drowned out by the sounds of their weapons discharging.

They fired at Switch again, but again he was too quick. Brick in hand, he sped toward the last car.

"The ice should have made this brittle enough by now," he assured himself as he slammed the brick into the passenger side door with enough speed to simulate an actual vehicle collision. With the wheels frozen in place, the car only moved a few inches, but the door broke free. He pulled it off its hinges and motioned to the two twenty-something women inside to quickly get out. Just as with the woman earlier, he scooped up the passenger as she got out and rushed her to safety, then came back and did the same for the driver.

"That's the last of you. Is everyone okay?" he double checked, surveying the roughly dozen and a half civilians he had pulled out of harm's way.

They were cold and they were scared, but everyone seemed to be okay. The effects of being trapped inside a tiny freezer without proper attire hadn't kicked in yet.

"Good," he said, satisfied that the people were unharmed. "Time for me to put these losers on ice."

In nothing but a motion blur, he was gone.

One of the women from the last car grimaced. "'Put these losers on ice'? Seriously?" she muttered through chattering teeth.

Switch raced around the corner, back to the henchmen. He came to a quick stop, the momentum still pulling his cape in the direction he was running.

"Hey, dorks!"

The henchmen, looking around in confusion a moment ago, now turned to him.

"Freeze," he said, a daring challenge.

With a slew of angry swears and insults, the six henchmen fired their freeze rays at him. Once again, they had no luck hitting the speedy sidekick. A tree, the side of a building, and a light pole all turned to ice instead of the person the criminals were actually trying to hit.

Switch moved around them, drawing their attention in all directions.

"Gotta make this quick," he said to himself, "before my powers give out!"

The criminals spread out as he zig zagged around them. The blur zipped between them and arced around them as they formed a defensive circle.

Switch appeared between them. He folded his arms and tapped his foot.

"We got him! Turn that brat into a popsicle!" shouted the leader of the group.

Six beams converged on Switch, only for him to speed away in the blink of an eye.

Six beams converged on six henchmen wielding ice guns.

"*Noooo!*" they cried as they hit each other with their own ice beams. Vapor in the air solidified, encasing them all in blocks of ice within seconds.

Switch appeared back between the frozen henchmen. "Too stupid to not form a circular firing squad. Crime doesn't pay, and neither did your college tuition. Oh, who am I kidding? Most of you probably didn't make it through high school."

That sound of battle down the block called for his attention. He heard a crash of metal and ice, along with an explosion.

In the distance was Blue Eagle, still battling the ice-armored Blizz Kid. They were engaged in a beam struggle, the superhero's red eyebeams clashing against the light blue beam of condensed frost and cold surging from the supervillain's outstretched hands. Neither gave ground to the other.

"It looks like Blue Eagle could use my help," noted Switch. He started to rush toward them, but stopped after a couple steps when he realized he wasn't moving at superspeed. "Huh. Or I guess I'll help him in about a minute. I hope one minute and not two."

He quickly rushed behind a parked car and observed the battle from the sidelines. He watched as the beams broke in Blizz Kid's favor. A shockwave of chilling air knocked Blue Eagle onto his back.

But it wasn't enough to keep the veteran superhero down. He glared daggers at the smirking Blizz Kid.

"Tell me, Blue Eagle. How does it feel to be so helpless against someone stronger than you?" taunted Blizz Kid, his words a cruel challenge.

"I don't know," muttered Blue Eagle, shooting to his feet. He lunged at Blizz Kid. "But I'll tell you if I ever find out!"

Blizz Kid's eyes glowed with anticipation. The ice at his wrists formed into swords. He swung as the superhero came within striking distance, but Blue Eagle stopped and nimbly dodged the attack.

"This is your end, you big blue pile of—"

"Language, Blizz Kid. Language," cautioned Blue Eagle, dodging another sword strike as he hovered inches above the ground. "Talking like that isn't going to make you not a joke among the rest of the city's villains."

"A joke? A *joke*!?" cried Blizz Kid. He swiped again and missed. Blue Eagle lacked the superspeed of his sidekick, but years of experience, not having to push off the ground to move while he was floating, and his focus on defense rather than risk-taking meant that he was skilled enough to dodge the teen's wild sword swings.

"To the other ice villains in the city. To the rest of *my* Rogues Gallery. A teenage ice villain? Come on," Blue Eagle replied coldly.

"You're just trying to get under my skin."

"Maybe. Or maybe not."

Blizz Kid growled. "I know what you're doing, Blue Eagle! And it won't work!" He slashed again, this time his blade slicing clean through a streetlight, causing it to slide off and fall to the pavement. "Other superheroes' ice villains respect me. Your villains respect me! The people of this city fear me! And I'll teach you to do the same!"

His swings were wild now, every movement using one hundred percent of his energy. And as they became more erratic, they became easier to dodge.

"You won't survive this, you generic cape-wearer," he threatened through gritted teeth. "I can make this armor light as a feather when it comes time to swing, and this blade thin enough to slice you in two."

"That means nothing if the person inside doesn't have what it takes to see it through. You're gassing out, Blizz Kid. And you'll never withstand a blow from me, armor or not."

Irritation flashed across the young supervillain's eyes. "I can increase the density of this armor far more than you....than you realize," he panted. He rushed toward Blue Eagle.

"Well, don't say I didn't try to give you any advice," said Blue Eagle nonchalantly, dodging another attack.

Switch watched as his father dodged more sword strikes. Blizz Kid's attacks grew more and more sloppy with each one.

He let out a huff under his breath. At least Blizz Kid could still use his powers. Switch was still in cooldown.

Blue Eagle dodged another wild but weak swing. "What's wrong, Blizz Kid? Getting tired?" he asked, like a father talking down to his son. "It must be hard for someone of normal strength to handle those split second moments where your gauntlets become strong enough to hurt even me."

Blizz Kid was panting hard at this point. "Shut up! Shut up, you...."

"You should cover your face," advised Blue Eagle, picking up the downed street light effortlessly, a feat that would shock anyone who didn't live in Herald City.

"....What?"

With a baseball player's swing, Blue Eagle slammed the lamppost into the young villain's chest. Chunks of crushed ice exploded into mist as the armor shattered.

The force of the blow sent Blizz Kid skidding back ten feet before he collapsed onto his stomach. He remained conscious, but laid on the ground panting heavily, his eyes wide open with shock.

"Had enough yet?" asked Blue Eagle tersely, tossing the lamppost aside.

Blizz Kid shakily pulled himself to one knee. He glared at his opponent. His lips curled into a snarl, ready to hurl a fiery insult.

Then he eyed Switch behind a car on the sidewalk, thinking he was unseen.

The corners of his mouth curled into a half smile.

"I'm shocked," he said, resting one hand on his knee. He surreptitiously moved his other hand behind his back. His breath was returning to him, but he played it up to throw Blue Eagle off guard. "I didn't think you'd get through my armor."

Blue Eagle's brow furrowed. He could tell Blizz Kid was up to something, but decided to play along. "You were too out of energy to make it dense enough to withstand that attack. You've always had a temper, Blizz Kid."

From behind the car, Switch felt his powers come back. And he also noticed Blizz Kid's hand behind his back.

"I admit, you got me on that, my old school nemesis," said Blizz Kid with a shrug. "I let you get under my skin."

Switch moved up to the next car, hoping the conversation would keep all eyes off him. From the better angle, he saw what Blizz Kid was doing.

An aura of icy air gathered quietly around the villain's fist. He was going to launch the attack when Blue Eagle's guard was down.

And there was no way to warn Blue Eagle without Blizz Kid just launching it.

He needed to get the drop on Blizz Kid, to take him down without being seen. And he needed to take him out with one decisive blow. Anything else would give Blizz Kid the chance to attack.

He flexed his bicep. His superstrength was activated. Quietly, he moved to the next car.

"What's your game, Blizz Kid?" demanded Blue Eagle. He stood straight with his hands on his hips, but turned to his side. He was ready to move at a moment's notice.

"My game? I'm short on petty cash," replied Blizz Kid sarcastically. "Could you spare a dollar to help a struggling youth?"

Switch moved to the next car. He was directly to Blizz Kid's right. Ahead of him was a tree wide enough to hide behind. He would be behind Blizz Kid then.

"Don't get snippy with me," warned Blue Eagle. "Your ambitions tend to be a lot bigger. What's your connection to Poster Boy's current crime spree?"

"Poster Boy? The only thing I'm doing to him is making him look like a chump in comparison. I mean, what is he going to do? Make armor out of poster papers? Out of himself? Just have a bunch of hims clinging to him like toddlers?"

Switch made it behind the tree and peered around. The sphere of ice around Blizz Kid's hidden hand was larger now, but calm. It was likely supposed to be a distraction so he could escape.

Keeping to a crouch, he stepped out behind the tree and started toward the villain. He wasn't about to let him make that escape.

"The whole 'clones climbing out of posters' thing is just a lame party trick he does for scares. He's just a psycho that thinks he's hot stuff," continued Blizz Kid. "I'm the best teen villain in your Rogues Gallery."

"The best? There's only three of you," argued Blue Eagle. He paused. "Which, now that I think about it, is actually an awful lot."

Switch was out in the open now. He glanced at Blue Eagle, who made eye contact for only an instant before refocusing on Blizz Kid. He was only a few yards away now.

Blizz Kid sneered. "It's strange that you have so many teen villains...."

He whirled around.

"....*when you no longer have a teen sidekick!*"

He fired a powerful arctic blast at Switch.

Chapter 16

Switch froze up.

Not literally. Not yet.

The concentrated blast of frost and wind barreled toward him faster than he could react, threatening to encase him in ice.

He didn't have time to wish he'd activated his speed instead of strength.

A pair of arms roughly wrapped around his waist and yanked him off the pavement. A yelp burst from his lips as he suddenly found himself moving sideways through the air.

Blue Eagle had already been moving when Blizz Kid fired his arctic blast. Because of that, he was able to fly past the supervillain and pull his son out of the way.

The wave of subzero temperature condensed into solid ice just as it passed where Switch had been standing. Like a light blue comet, the icy blast splintered the tree and continued through the building behind it, slamming through multiple storefronts in multiple properties. Brick, concrete, and plaster turned to ice just before tearing to pieces.

When it was all done, there was an open path from one corner of the building to the next. Icicles dripping water arced over the trail of destruction.

Blue Eagle had had enough. He fired his eyebeam directly into Blizz Kid's chest. The beam wasn't nearly his full power; that would have been fatal. But it was powerful enough that—with the ice armor gone—the teen was blasted off his feet, landing in a crumpled heap on his side.

A soft moan escaped the young villain's lips as he laid on the ground, smoke wafting from his chest. Behind his ski goggles, his eyes fluttered closed.

Blizz Kid was defeated.

"I think Blizz Kid's been *put on ice*," quipped Switch as his father released him. He thought for a second. "No, wait, I think I used that one already."

"What about the civilians? And his henchmen?" asked Blue Eagle.

"I took care of them all. The people are around the corner, unharmed. The bad guys are cooling off," answered Switch with a tiny smirk.

"Good," said Blue Eagle with a nod. He cast a side eyed glare at his sidekick. "But you shouldn't be making jokes after the stunt you just pulled."

Switch blinked in confusion. He was taken so completely by surprise by the statement that he didn't even know what to respond to, let alone how to respond.

"I.... What do you mean?" he finally managed to ask.

"What do you mean what do I mean?" replied Blue Eagle forcefully, his voice raising in frustration. "What were you thinking, creeping up behind Blizz Kid like that when he's powering up a giant ice blast?"

"The….I…." stammered Switch. He didn't know how to respond. He always hesitated when put on the spot like this.

How was it that he was able to rush headfirst into danger against superpowered criminals but couldn't handle a dressing down from his father?

"I just… I was gonna sneak attack him from behind…." he eventually squeaked, his voice not much louder than a whisper. His plan suddenly felt like the stupidest thing ever thought up by someone in tights and a cape.

"You were going to *sneak attack* him from behind? Switch, you're a superhero, not a ninja! You don't know how to do stealth! Tell me, what type of stealth has you tiptoeing like a character from a 1960s cartoon in broad view of everyone, including the person that's going to blast you into next week?"

Switch's mind hunted for a response. One that would not prompt an unassailable counterargument from his father.

His face grew hot as he realized he had nothing to say as a result.

After a few seconds listening to nothing but the rare "Uhh" and "Umm", Blue Eagle shook his head. "Of course you didn't think of that! Look at what that blast did."

He pointed to the impact point of Blizz Kid's final attack. They could see all the way to the next street.

"What were you planning to do if I wasn't here to pull you out of the way?"

Switch looked at the damaged building, then turned back to his father. "I had superstrength activated. So I would have probably tanked that blast...."

There wasn't any confidence in his voice as those words left his lips, and he regretted not giving *any* other answer.

Blue Eagle just stared blankly at his sidekick, then shook his head in disbelief. "*I* wouldn't want to get hit by that," was his only reply, gesturing again at the damaged building.

"But I'm stronger than you when I activate superstrength," blurted Switch, immediately regretting it.

Blue Eagle raised an eyebrow, glaring at his son. Switch looked away. That line of argument was now closed.

Eventually, Blue Eagle turned toward Blizz Kid's unconscious body. "Now that we've settled that, Switch, why don't you call the....police...."

His voice trailed off as he noticed something.

"What's wrong? What is it?" asked Switch, taking out his phone.

Blue Eagle's brow furrowed as he stepped closer to Blizz Kid. He knelt down as he inspected the back of the villain's neck.

It was so small that he would never have noticed it without his enhanced vision.

There was a tiny red spot about a quarter of a millimeter in diameter on the back of Blizz Kid's neck.

It looked like it would have come from a syringe. But on the back of the neck? That made no sense.

Of course, it could have just been a rash, or from the battle, or from the constant ice generation. It could have been from the armor he'd been wearing.

He could have just scratched it too hard.

Still....

He looked over at Switch, one eyebrow raised, weighing different possibilities and wondering whether they were worth addressing.

"Blue Eagle, what is it?" repeated Switch.

No, it wasn't worth the time. It was just a tiny red spot.

And they had more pressing matters at hand.

"Nothing. Don't mind me," he said, getting to his feet. "Call the police and let them know it's safe to pick up Blizz Kid. Then let's go take down Poster Boy."

Chapter 17

The Father-Son Duo were in the air again, flying to Poster Boy's location. They didn't have to wait too long for the HCPD to come to pick up Blizz Kid as the surrounding streets had been evacuated during the fight.

It wouldn't be too long before they arrived in Highland Heights, where Poster Boy clones were running amok.

Like before, and like always, Blue Eagle held Switch around his waist. The teen grunted as he shifted uncomfortably.

"What's wrong?" asked Blue Eagle, noticing his son squirming around.

"Nothing. Just trying to get into a more comfortable position," said Switch, shifting again. "It's tough flying the way we do."

"That's because you can't fly on your own without risking falling out of the sky," reminded Blue Eagle, adjusting his grip so that Switch would be more comfortable.

"I know," sighed Switch, his expression darkening. He watched the buildings pass by below.

"That's why I have to fight crime like this. So we can arrive at a crime scene at the same time with your powers ready to go so you can help out."

"I know," repeated Switch, the exasperation evident in his voice.

Blue Eagle raised an eyebrow. "Someone's grouchy today," he remarked. "I know it's embarrassing to be carried around by your father like this, but there's nothing else we can do unless you want to skydive into battle without a parachute. I would say you can try landing on the supervillain, but that would only work once," he added with a fatherly chuckle.

Switch stifled a sigh. Even a faint huff would have been heard by Blue Eagle's enhanced hearing.

He let his eyes trace over the maze of streets far below. He wished he was down there. He hated when his power deficiencies were brought up. Even if Blue Eagle was right.

Especially because Blue Eagle was right.

His phone vibrated. He pulled it out and saw the incoming text from Jasper. He brought up the full text and read it. Then he read it again, not believing what he read the first time.

switch, its jasper. the highlad heights robberies is a distraction!!

poster boy has his guys planting a bomb in subway in midtown

Switch's breath caught in his throat. A bomb in the Herald City Subway? Thousands of people were in the Midtown station alone at any given time.

The results of a bomb going off there would be catastrophic!

"What's wrong?" asked Blue Eagle, noticing his sudden concern. A hopeful grin spread across his face. "Is it a girl from school?"

"No, I...." started Switch, eliciting a disappointed groan from Blue Eagle. He paused when he realized he couldn't tell his father *where* he got the information from.

His mind worked feverishly as he spoke. "I, uh, just got a news alert on my phone that Poster Boy's henchmen were spotted setting up a bomb in the Midtown subway station!" he reported.

Blue Eagle stopped short. Switch grasped his father's arm as he lurched forward.

"Are you sure?" asked Blue Eagle.

Switch nodded. "I'm sure," he answered, hoping his father wouldn't ask to see the "news alert".

"Midtown Station is nearby," said Blue Eagle. He glanced in the direction of the tallest buildings of the Herald City skyline, which included the Powers Industries headquarters, the TomorrowTech Industries research building, and the clawlike SPIRE Tower. Midtown Herald City. "Catching Poster Boy will have to wait. We have to stop that bomb!" he exclaimed, taking off toward the station as fast as he could.

Within minutes, they touched down in front of the subway entrance. Blue Eagle let go of Switch and, together, the two superheroes raced downstairs. They quickly passed people checking train schedules and leaving fare control, and headed toward the ticket booth.

"Excuse me," said Blue Eagle, tapping on the glass to get the ticket agent's attention.

The bored ticket agent didn't look up from her phone. "Sir, the schedule is on that screen over there," she huffed and pointed in the general direction of a ticker showing the train arrival and departure times.

Blue Eagle and Switch exchanged glances. Switch just shook his head.

"Excuse me," repeated Blue Eagle, tapping on the glass again. "It's urgent."

The employee glanced up, and her eyes widened with shock at the sight of the two superheroes standing outside her booth. "Blue Eagle and Switch!" she exclaimed, putting her phone down and sitting upright. "Oh my—W-what can I do for you?"

"Contact your superiors. Tell them to shut down all trains and lock down this station. There's a bomb planted somewhere!"

Police tape covered the entrance to the Midtown subway station entrance. Police officers kept reporters and curious onlookers at bay.

Inside, a group of officers in specialized uniforms—one carrying a metal briefcase—emerged from the subway tunnel and approached Blue Eagle, Switch, and a handful of police officers who were waiting on the platform.

"Lieutenant, we've searched the whole tunnel. We found nothing," reported the bomb squad team leader.

"Nothing?" echoed the lieutenant in a shock shared by both the other officers and the superheroes.

"Nothing. I don't think there's a bomb down here."

"You're sure?"

"Yeah. We've just spent the last three hours searching the station and the tunnels quite thoroughly. We've seen no Poster Boy henchmen, no sign of equipment tampering, and we haven't detected any unusual chemical substances either in the air or on any surface." The bomb squad leader turned to Blue Eagle. "You've also been through these tunnels and you've smelled nothing with your enhanced senses?"

"Correct," confirmed Blue Eagle.

"You used your superspeed to search quickly through the station and both tunnels?" the bomb squad leader confirmed with Switch.

"Twice," said Switch. "And I even went to the next stops in both directions."

"There's no bomb," the bomb squad leader said pointedly to the lieutenant. "It must have been some prankster calling a fake bomb threat for fun."

"We didn't get an anonymous call, though," countered the lieutenant. "Blue Eagle was the one who found out about it."

"We weren't the ones to uncover the bomb threat. Switch got a news alert on his phone, and we rushed here right away," clarified Blue Eagle.

"A news alert? Impossible. There's been no information in the media about this since we shut down the subway," said the lieutenant.

Switch's mind raced. "No, I got an alert from the police scanner app," he lied.

Blue Eagle paused for a beat. "Excuse us, officers. Switch and I are going to go strategize for a moment," he told the cops.

He patted Switch's back and guided him away from the officers, to the other side of the platform.

Switch's heart raced. He knew he was in trouble. He could feel the forcefulness of his father's hand behind his back. It wasn't rough or painful, but he could notice the ever-so-slight amount of enhanced strength pressing against his upper back. That meant Blue Eagle meant business.

When they were out of earshot of the officers, Blue Eagle released his grip and folded his arms, glaring sternly at Switch.

"Where did you get that there was a bomb threat on the subway system?" he asked firmly.

"I saw it on my phone," said Switch meekly, his shoulders hunched slightly.

"Show me."

"Uh, wh-what?"

"Show me," repeated Blue Eagle. "I want to see the exact thing on your phone that said there was a bomb on the subway."

Switch began to mentally panic. "I, uh, don't think I could find it again. I didn't save it," he said. His eyes darted around as if some escape hatch would get him out of this situation.

"Unlock your phone and give it to me," ordered Blue Eagle, holding his hand out.

Switch hesitated, not sure what to do.

"You can either unlock your phone and give it to me for a few minutes or I can take it from you locked and not give it back at all," said Blue Eagle sternly, the weight of his glare almost enough to bore through his sidekick's head.

There was no getting out of this one. With a hand that felt like it was weighed down with lead, he took his phone out of his belt pouch. He slowly, painfully typed his passcode in to unlock the phone, then reluctantly handed it to his father.

Blue Eagle scrolled through the phone for all of two seconds before his brow furrowed. He turned the phone toward Switch.

It was the text from Jasper. Switch had left his text messages open.

"So it's from this Jasper character that you got the bomb threat," said Blue Eagle. "Who is this 'Jasper'? One of your friends from school?"

"It's....just someone I know," answered Switch nervously.

"I'm sure," muttered Blue Eagle sarcastically. He scrolled up, and his lips pressed together as his eyes widened with anger. "Jasper is a criminal."

He looked up at Switch. "He's a criminal! One of Poster Boy's henchmen!" he shouted at the teen. "How long have you been in contact with this criminal!?"

"Only recently," replied Switch, his voice tiny and soft.

Blue Eagle slapped his thigh in frustration. "You're really giving me detailed answers right now," he hissed sarcastically. "How long. Have you. Been in contact. With this criminal?"

Switch swallowed hard. "I.... Only since we stopped Poster Boy from kidnapping the mayor."

"He's one of the henchmen of the villain that tried to kidnap the mayor! And it sounds like he was present at the kidnapping attempt and is probably helping out with Poster Boy's big crime spree up in Highland Heights! The spree we completely failed to stop! I hope that one of the other superheroes did! Tell me, what possessed you to *consort* with this criminal!?"

"I....I mean...." sputtered Switch. He wished this conversation would just end already. He hated being yelled at so *so* much. "H-he didn't want to be a criminal. So he was giving me information....from the inside."

"Really," said Blue Eagle sarcastically. "This is why none of that stuff you read about fixing the 'system' and whatever else is going to change these people. Criminals can go get jobs if they don't want to be criminals. Jasper wants to be a criminal because it's easier to take money that isn't yours than it is to go out and earn it. And it's the job of us superheroes to make them realize that—what? What's the old line about crime?"

"That crime doesn't pay," mumbled Switch.

"That's right. Or at least it doesn't when superheroes are *catching* the criminals and not chatting with them." Blue Eagle pointed to the phone. "Is this where you were getting all that stuff earlier about Liberty Park?"

Switch reluctantly nodded.

Blue Eagle closed his eyes and sighed, his nose scrunching with frustration.

"Again. Jasper was trying to trick you into being somewhere else when the real supervillain schemes went off. And I wonder how many times you would have fallen for it," he admonished, handing the phone back to Switch. He placed a firm hand on the boy's shoulder, nudging him back toward the cops. "Come," he demanded harshly.

Together, they walked briskly back across the platform. To Switch, the ten second trip seemed to take multiple long, agonizing minutes. He wondered if there was someone with time manipulation powers making things take longer.

"Excuse me, Lieutenant," called Blue Eagle pleasantly as they approached the officers. "My apologies. This was all our fault. We were given bad information by a thug we interrogated. But we're on our way to get to the bottom of the *real* villainous scheme going down."

The lieutenant glanced at the other officers and nodded. "I understand, it happens," he said. He tipped his hat at the superheroes. "Go knock 'em dead."

"We will, Lieutenant. We will," promised Blue Eagle. When he turned around, the pleasant look was gone.

He shot Switch a dirty look as he gave the boy's arm a rough tug, and together they left the subway station.

In the Highland Heights neighborhood, a Hispanic girl in purple tights and a flowing cloak blasted a Poster Boy clone with a beam of concentrated darkness.

"That's another down," said Night Girl as the poster clone vanished.

A black teenager in red armor, with an eyepiece screen over his left eye and the TomorrowTech Industries logo on his chest, slashed another poster clone in half with a pink hard-light sword emitted from his metal gauntlet.

"Only one more to go," reported Bionic Boy, watching as the two halves disappeared bloodlessly.

A woman dressed as a cheetah leapt on top of the last poster clone. Her claws ripped through its chest.

"And we're done," sighed The Cheetah From Charon, disappointed at the lack of blood the vanishing clone produced.

The three superheroes looked around. The people had run for their lives earlier. There had been no one but clones of Poster Boy when they got there.

Now there wasn't even that. The posters and pictures that lined the stores and billboards were back to normal. Wherever Poster Boy had been, he was gone now.

"I guess that's it," said Night Girl. "I know Poster Boy's personality. He wouldn't stop unless he thought he lost. Which means he either is hiding, or he ran off. Probably the latter."

"We should search for him just in case," said The Cheetah From Charon. "These fakes do not bleed. And I crave his blood, even if he is the enemy of another superhero."

"Okay, but that brings up another question," said Night Girl, taking a step away from the other hero. "Where are Blue Eagle and Switch? Poster Boy is one of *their* villains. Why aren't they dealing with this?"

"There was a bomb threat at the Herald City Subway station in Midtown," said Bionic Boy, looking at data that scrolled over his eyepiece. "The bigger question I have is what was the point of all *this*?"

At that moment, across town, a group of men wearing black clothing and face-covering bandanas exited a charity gala carrying burlap sacks and automatic weapons. They hooted and hollered triumphantly as they jumped into the black van parked out front.

"Good haul, boys. Good haul," congratulated Clay as he ripped off his bandana, settling into the front passenger's seat.

"Yeah. All that loot stolen from these snooty rich folks at this charity whatever thing and no interference from any capes," said one of the thugs behind him, patting his bag proudly.

"We can thank our boy Clemens here for that," laughed Clay, reaching over to the driver's seat and patting Jasper on the shoulder. "It was his idea to send the eagles on a wild goose chase through the subway."

"Hey, do eagles actually eat geese?" asked another crook.

Jasper laughed. "That's what that kid gets for trusting me."

"You know, I actually thought the worst when you told us you were speaking to Switch the Blue Eaglet," said Clay. He grinned. "But I was wrong. You ain't a stool pigeon, Clemens. You came through."

"Hey, don't worry about it. You guys know I'm in all the way."

The men laughed and went back to looking through all the wallets, purses, and jewelry they stole. Jasper turned away to begin driving, and no one saw the look of pain and defeat that flashed across his face.

Chapter 18

Blue Eagle flew slow and low over the city, once again carrying Switch with him.

And this time was particularly unpleasant.

Switch felt ridiculous as people looked up to see them flying only a few yards over the two and three story buildings of that neighborhood. Everyone could see them clearly because they were flying so low. And because of the slow speed, his legs were dangling awkwardly below him rather than stretched out behind him.

The tension between him and his father was thick enough right now that Switch could probably swim through it.

Right now, he just felt shame and embarrassment. He had been a superhero since he was 12. He wasn't a kid anymore! He was 15! How could he let Jasper trick him like that? How *could* Jasper trick him like that? His story seemed genuine. Was he being coerced? Did Queen Venus mindjack him? Did he even send those texts?

For a moment, he wondered if the whole Queen Venus-Planticite-Treescraper plot was even real. Part of him hoped it was, just so he could feel *slightly* less stupid.

But what if it *was*?

Not that there was anything he could do about it now. Blue Eagle would never believe him if he explained it. And Switch was probably going to be grounded until he was 25, so there was no way he could investigate on his own. And who could he get to do it on his behalf? No one, likely, after he accidentally called in a *fake bomb threat* and shut down half the Herald City Subway system.

After another moment, Blue Eagle finally broke the silence. "I'm so disappointed in you right now, Switch. So disappointed," he said with a heavy sight.

Breaking the silence did not mean breaking the tension. Switch said nothing, hoping the conversation would just end itself.

"What were you thinking?" asked Blue Eagle harshly, not letting the conversation end itself.

There was a pause as Switch didn't have an answer. But an angry grunt from Blue Eagle made it clear that it wasn't a rhetorical question.

"I was just trying to help," he answered tepidly, less a rationalization and more an appeal for understanding.

"What part of acting on false information from crooks and villain henchmen was 'helping'?" pressed Blue Eagle. "It's one thing to be into all that liberal nonsense about being soft on criminals or whatever, but this? Going behind my back like this? I trusted you! I had the cops shut down the subway based on your word!"

"I'm sorry," whispered Switch, wanting desperately right now to be in any situation other than this one.

"Oh, you definitely will be. You're sitting this one out. I'll take down Poster Boy on my own, and you're going to be grounded until the next generation of superheroes emerges."

They finally landed in front of the Herald City Police Headquarters.

"What are we doing here?" asked Switch as Blue Eagle released him.

Blue Eagle said nothing. He just started toward the building.

"What are we doing at the HCPD?" asked Switch again. A sudden fear washed over him. "Are....are you having me arrested?"

"Of course not!" snapped Blue Eagle. "But you're going to tell the cops everything about this criminal you're in cahoots with, and then you're going to go home and wait there until I get back so we can talk more about this."

Switch followed his father into the precinct, trying as best he could not to look dejected as they passed by the many police officers and administrative staff going about their jobs. His stomach tightened with dread as he realized where he was being led.

Within a couple of minutes, they were in front of the office door of the Chief of Police.

"Chief? It's Blue Eagle and Switch. The receptionist said you were in," announced Blue Eagle, knocking softly on the door.

There was no response. But Blue Eagle's ears picked up a faint sigh on the other end.

"Chief? You in there?" he called again, his knuckles softly tapping against the wooden door again. He turned the knob and opened the door.

The Chief's office was fairly big. A large oak desk stood in the center of the room, and pictures of himself in the Police Academy and on the beat lined the walls. There was a large window overlooking the courtyard on one side of the room.

The Chief stood with his back to the window. The sun's rays illuminated him and his desk as if they were centerpieces of a museum exhibit.

"Chief?" uttered Blue Eagle.

From when they came in until a brief second after Blue Eagle got his attention, the Chief seemed to be staring into nothing. He then blinked and glanced over at the superheroes.

"Blue Eagle! Switch!" he exclaimed, his usual gruff self. He stood in the light of the window, the sun shining in the back of his head and neck. "It's about darned time you two got your spandexed behinds in here!"

Switch frowned. The Chief seemed normal enough—this was his bad mood self—but something still seemed off. Something was wrong.

"How are you doing, Chief?" asked Blue Eagle politely, already knowing the answer.

"How am I doing!? Terrible!" the Chief shot back. He stomped right up to the superhero. "You mind telling me why you had *my* police dealing with the subway and not the charity gala?"

"What charity gala?" asked Switch.

"The one Poster Boy's men robbed blind while I had officers trying to stop his rampage through Highland Heights!?" the Chief practically shouted.

Switch winced. He could feel his father's glare on him.

"I didn't have enough officers to fight back against all those Poster Boy clones he had jumping out of all the posters there! Luckily, we had a few superheroes that decided to lend a hand," continued the Chief. "We were so busy with that that we had no idea about the gala heist until it was too late."

Blue Eagle gave Switch a deliberate pat on the back. "Switch can explain one, Chief. I'm going to go out and help stop Poster Boy."

"Oh, he got away. There's nothing for you to do now, Blue Eagle, so you might as well go home."

"Well, that's disappointing," said Blue Eagle. "Still, the least I can do right now I'd try to pick up his trail. Wherever he's hiding, he won't stay hidden for long."

"Don't worry about it, Blue Eagle. I've got detectives working the case already. Like I said, you can just go home now. You've done more than enough stopping the Blizz Kid rampage."

Switch raised an eyebrow. "Wow, I never thought I'd see the day where the Chief of Police tells Blue Eagle he isn't needed," he remarked.

"Uhh.... Be that as it may, it's worth a try...." said Blue Eagle, his voice trailing off. His brow knitted in confusion. He took a step forward. "Chief, it's possible we may be dealing with a villain team up. Blizz Kid's attack might have been a distraction for whatever Poster Boy was trying to accomplish."

"Duly noted," acknowledged the Chief. "But it's more likely to be a coincidence. I can't imagine those two egos working together."

"Have the police spoken to these gala attendees?" asked Switch, quickly scrolling through his phone.

"Of course," confirmed the Chief.

"According to the breaking news covering it, the gala was robbed by a group of armed men. But no connection between them and any larger group was confirmed," reported Switch, reading the report.

"Okay, you can go over this with the Chief after you tell him all the information you've *collected* recently," said Blue Eagle sternly, patting Switch's shoulder in a way that meant "Stop talking".

"So you've spoken to the gala attendees?" confirmed Switch.

"Of course," replied the Chief with a chuckle. "They identified Poster Boy as the ringleader."

"'Officers on the scene collected witness statements. So far, the HCPD and the gala attendees interviewed directly by reporters have stated that the men were unidentified'," read Switch, his heart racing. He couldn't believe he was challenging the Chief like this.

"That's enough," demanded Blue Eagle. "Why don't you tell the Chief all about that criminal you were getting your so-called *information* from while I go find Poster Boy?"

He started toward the door, then turned around. He saw Switch, eyes cast downward, and felt something gnawing softly at him. A hunch.

Perhaps a hunch not worth pursuing, but a hunch nonetheless.

Why not?

"After I'm done with Poster Boy, I want to check out something at Liberty Park," he informed the Chief.

Switch's eyes lifted suddenly. A surprised but relieved and hopeful look spread across his face.

The Chief didn't look as hopeful. In fact, he looked worried. "Why? What's wrong?"

"Nothing major," assured Blue Eagle. "But with all that's going on, I want to make sure Mayor Warren's construction project is going fine."

"Understandable, but I wouldn't worry, Blue Eagle. Your attention there isn't necessary."

"I'm sure it isn't, but it doesn't hurt to follow up on some leads."

The Chief gave a sharp laugh. "That's nonsense!" he exclaimed. He thought for a moment. "You both had leads to share with me involving criminal activity? Sit down. Let's take some time and go over it."

He turned to pull out the two chairs in front of his desk so they could sit. As he did so, Blue Eagle's super vision saw it.

Tiny, almost imperceptible. On the back of the Chief's neck.

It was a mark. Less than a millimeter in diameter, surrounded by the faintest of red skin.

Just like on the back of Blizz Kid's neck.

He frowned as the Chief stepped to the side, gesturing for the heroes to sit down.

"I'm not needed for that, and I'm going to begin my search," he told the Chief, shaking his head. "In fact, I'm going to have Switch join me on this."

Switch kept his face mostly still, save for the slight widening of his eyes and cocking of his head as he realized that Blue Eagle also knew something was wrong with the Chief.

And then the image errantly popped into his mind. The sight of Clay doing that weird neck touch to the Chief when hooking up his mic.

Planticites. Parasites that hijack the mind.

It all clicked.

The Chief had been mindjacked! He was now an extension of Queen Venus.

For all intent and purpose, they were talking to Queen Venus!

The Chief glanced at both heroes. "I'm going to insist you stay away from Liberty Park," he told them. "If you really are concerned about suspicious goings-on over there, I can contact the Defending Champions and ask them to check it out."

"The Defending Champions?" echoed Blue Eagle incredulously. "I think sending the world's top superhero team to investigate 'nothing' is a tad overkill, isn't it? Switch and I will check it out after we search for Poster Boy."

"No! I....I absolutely *insist* you both stay right here in this building!" demanded the Chief.

Blue Eagle's eyes narrowed. "What are you hiding, Chief? Tell me right now," he ordered, crossing his arms.

"How....*dare* you accuse—"

"Queen Venus is implanting parasites into the back of certain people's necks to make them part of her plant collective!" blurted Switch, interrupting the Chief's ranting.

Both men stared at him. A look of rage and panic flashed across the Chief's face. It was a confirmation of everything he was saying.

"The mayor and a bunch of city officials are already under her control. So are Blizz Kid and Poster Boy," he continued. "She's working on something at the Liberty Park construction site that will put all of Herald City under her control!"

Blue Eagle was dumbfounded. He looked back and forth between the others, as if trying to determine if he really just heard what he heard.

The Chief was more decisive. He quickly pulled out his radio and pressed the talk button. "All officers to my office immediately!" he ordered. "Blue Eagle and Switch have gone rogue! All officers to my office to place Blue Eagle and Switch under arrest!"

He drew his gun and pointed it at Blue Eagle.

"Chief! What are you—" started the startled superhero.

"Die, you meddling cape!" interrupted the Chief, aiming at Blue Eagle's chest.

Switch was already on the move. He tanked the hit—the bullet bouncing harmlessly off his invulnerable body—and grabbed at the gun. The Chief was stronger than him, but wasn't prepared for a knee to the gut. Weakened, the Chief couldn't stop Switch from wrenching the pistol out of his hand and hitting him in the back of the head with it, knocking him out.

There was a pause as Switch looked over the Chief's unconscious form. He then turned to Blue Eagle, who stood motionless, mouth slightly agape.

"What!? You saw what happened!" protested Switch. "He went right for excessive force for an unlawful arrest! I was only defending myself!"

Blue Eagle quickly shook his head, as if snapping out of a trance. "Oh no, I completely agree. It's just that—"

The door burst open as multiple officers entered with guns drawn. Switch suddenly became painfully aware of the fact that he was standing over the unconscious body of the Chief of Police in his own office holding a gun that everyone had heard discharge.

"I....uh...." he started.

"It's true! Blue Eagle and Switch *have* gone rogue!" cried a cop. "Take 'em down!"

It was an ordinary day for anyone outside the police headquarters in Herald City.

That is, until a pair of superheroes burst out a window, gunfire whizzing past their ears.

"I was gonna say, it's just that when you have a mind controlled person of authority coming at you with a gun, don't do anything to make it look like *you're* the bad guy!" advised Blue Eagle as they ran across the courtyard.

"I'll keep that in mind," said Switch sarcastically, a bullet bouncing harmlessly off the back of his head.

They made it across the grassy field and dived over an empty police cruiser parked at the curb.

"Alright, you're the one who knows all about whatever's going on here. Where are we going?" asked Blue Eagle as they took cover behind the cruiser.

"The Liberty Park construction site," said Switch over the sound of bullets bouncing off the car. "Apparently, everything with Blizz Kid and Poster Boy has been a distraction. Queen Venus has been working in the shadows to get everything she needs to build a giant tree skyscraper there."

"You sure?"

"I'm positive. Blizz Kid and Poster Boy are under her control right now, just like the Chief. Why else would they be holding dual crime sprees at the exact same time if it wasn't to divert our attention away from her? She's doing something big right now, I know it."

Blue Eagle frowned. "That's a bit over the top, even for her. But it should take a long time to build an entire building, so we should have plenty of time to stop her."

The ground started shaking. The police stopped firing at them and looked off into the distance in shock.

Everyone looked off into the distance in shock.

A tree trunk rocketed out of the ground far across the city. It grew wider and wider and taller and taller every second. Branches burst from the trunk, like the arms of people breaking free of a trap, and those branches sprouted other branches. Tens of new branches per second, then hundreds. Leaves sprouted from the branches, hundreds per second, then thousands. All as the tree grew taller and taller.

"Whoa," breathed the awestruck Switch.

"Yeah. Whoa," echoed Blue Eagle, his jaw hanging open.

A shadow covered the city like a blanket. Ordinary people and superheroes alike stopped what they were doing and stared in awe as the foliage cast a shade over everything.

A muscular superhero in black tights with a scarred face and exposed left chest and arm swore as he watched the giant tree form above him, his machete held dangerously close to the violent gang member he had pinned in the alley.

The humanoid lioness in pink tights with a short white cape and lion head insignia on her chest stood on the roof of a building, awestruck by the act of unnatural nature she saw before her.

Multiple flying superheroes had to quickly adjust their flight path to avoid being caught in the expanding foliage.

When all was said and done, the tree stood three times as tall as SPIRE Tower, the tallest building in the city. Its shadow covered all of Herald City, night enveloping everything.

"Is that what you were expecting?" asked Blue Eagle.

"No," said Switch. "Not quite *that*."

The control room was unusually bright for a room made entirely of wood. The floor and walls were uneven, just like the exterior of the massive tree. Along one side of the room were hollows, all about the length and width of a human arm and all appearing in pairs.

Queen Venus entered the control room, followed reluctantly by a group of henchmen.

Among them was Jasper Clemens.

One henchman nudged the person next to him. "Man, being part of a building literally growing itself into existence was a heck of a rush!"

"I hope Queen Venus built or grew bathrooms in this thing, because I might have to throw up after that," said the other crook, his face contorting with disgust.

"Enough talk," huffed Queen Venus as she stood by the hollows. She pointed at the two men and a third one near them. "You, you, and you. Place your arms into these tree hollows."

The three men looked at each other in confusion, the rest of the group cautiously stepping away from them. "Uh, you want us....to....?" started one of them.

"Put. Your arms. Into these tree hollows," she repeated forcefully. When they hesitated, she bellowed, "Do you wish to anger me, worms? Do you wish to challenge me? Or do you wish to obey?"

Reluctantly, the three henchmen chose obedience. They cautiously approached the hollows.

"You need not worry. I didn't keep you around all this time just to senselessly slaughter you," she assured them. "I would have senselessly slaughtered you a long time ago if you weren't needed to operate the controls of the Treescraper."

The henchmen gave one last hesitant look at Clay, who stood next to the larger group like a dog herding sheep. He gave them a stern nod, as if frustrated by their hesitation. With no other option, they placed their arms inside the hollows, all the way to the elbows.

They cried out as vines connected to their fingertips, wrapped around their hands, and snaked up their arms.

A single vine made it to each side of their heads. Suction cup feelers attached to the sides of their temples. The men gasped as they felt their minds become part of the tree.

"Whoa! This is intense!"

"I feel like....like I can *control* everything! This whole tree building!"

"A portion of the *Treescraper*, yes. To the degree that I allow," confirmed Queen Venus. "While I can control plants, there is a ceiling to what I can do at any time. But with the Photosynthesis Enhancer and some other materials, I was able to build this massive fortress of nature on the site my city officials kindly set up for me, and manufacture Planticites at a rate I couldn't possibly achieve on my own. Do you feel the branches and leaves as if they were an extension of your arms?"

Two of the men nodded. The other murmured a confirmation.

"Those leaves function as lenses for sunlight. They will help you distribute the Planticites. The Treescraper is producing the last of them now," she continued.

She turned to the group. "You've all played your parts well. As I instructed, Poster Boy and Blizz Kid led simultaneous attacks on the city, drawing the attention of the authorities and the superheroes so all the materials and equipment could be brought here without raising suspicion. Some of your comrades, including Blizz Kid, were defeated and are no doubt on their way to jail, but that will be quickly rectified. I keep you alive and your minds uninfected so you can interface with the Treescraper and execute its higher functions while my powers are spread thin. Be grateful for this privilege."

No one had the courage to speak up and thank her for the "privilege".

She turned back to the three henchmen interfacing with the Treescraper.

"Speaking of executing, it's time. Distribute the Planticites!" she ordered. She clenched her fist. "Make Herald City my kingdom! At long last, make Herald City *mine!*"

Her maniacal laughter bouncing off the wooden walls was the first thing that gave Jasper the chills. The second was watching the three henchmen's eyes close and suddenly shoot open, their pupils dilated as they interfaced with the natural computer.

He felt the back of his neck and was grateful to be one of the useful few spared a terrible fate.

Remembering how cruel fate had been to him his whole life, though, perhaps this was how it should be.

Foliage shifted. Millions of leaves high above Herald City deliberately faced specifically chosen directions. Sunlight from above gently touched them, shining through and diverging as it did so.

Tiny bugs crawled out of the pores in the branches. They were nearly invisible to anyone who would have been watching. They looked more like dust mites than anything.

They were the Planticites.

They had small, rounded bodies with sharp feelers for mouths.

They crawled over and through the thick, but porous leaves, their bodies tiny enough to maneuver through holes most people wouldn't have noticed. They clung to the bottoms of these leaves, which were specially engineered to focus light.

The leaves reoriented. Rather than diverging, the beams of light shining through converged. The sudden movement of heat and energy was enough to carry the tiny creatures.

Millions of beams of focused light seem to fire from the foliage like lasers, each carrying with them a mind-altering parasite. The parasites seemed to absorb the light, attracting it as they maneuvered toward their targets.

Millions of parasites targeted each of Herald City's millions of residents.

People didn't feel pain as faint beams of light spun off and seemed to curve, hitting them in the backs of their necks. Man, woman, and child, superhero and supervillain, on the ground or in flight, all curiously touched the backs of their necks as they felt a slight flash of warmth.

Blue Eagle and Switch watched helplessly as the beams of light hit the back of each police officer's neck. The cops stood there in confusion, wondering what on Earth they were witnessing.

Then Blue Eagle turned and saw two more beams of light coming right toward him and Switch.

"Switch, move!" he shouted, grabbing the teen and diving back over the cop car.

The pair of intense beams grazed across the top of the vehicle, coming too close to the heroes for their comfort.

Blue Eagle shot upright. "Switch, are you okay? Were you hit?" he asked frantically.

Switch pulled himself up to his hands and knees. His eyes suddenly went wide. "I think that hit," he breathed, feeling the back of his neck. "I felt a quick flash of heat, I think right here."

His father pushed his head down, inspecting the back of his neck.

"I saw the tiniest red mark on the back of Blizz Kid's neck earlier, and the Chief's a few minutes ago. Like something tiny had burrowed into their skin, something so small they wouldn't have even noticed," explained Blue Eagle. After a quick inspection, he sighed in relief and patted his son on the back. "I think you're fine."

"I'm not surprised. I still had my invulnerability up," said Switch, his words masking the relief he felt. That was too close. "Did you get hit?"

"Thankfully no," said Blue Eagle. "What just happened now, was that what you were warning me about? The thing that's supposed to put all of Herald City under Queen Venus's control?"

"I think so. I'm pretty sure," answered Switch. "Jasper said that the Treescraper would be able to transport the mind control parasites–*Planticites*, he called them–through sunlight into the back of people's necks. Supposedly, anyone infected becomes essentially one of Queen Venus's plants."

"After what happened with the Chief, that sounds about right," remarked Blue Eagle. "But what about the rest of the city?"

"Blue Eagle!"

They turned at the sound of the police officers from before approaching them. On the street, people approached the cops and the superheroes in confusion.

"Officers, I hope you understand that we don't have time for this. We need to–" started Blue Eagle.

"No, no. We understand. You didn't attack the Chief. His mind was hijacked by *that* giant thing," interrupted one of the officers, pointing toward the Treescraper.

"Good to hear. Now, I suggest you let these people know that everything is going to be alright. Switch and I are on the case!"

"That won't be necessary, Blue Eagle. They're all aware of what's going on. And you're not going anywhere," said the officer.

Blue Eagle and Switch looked around. The people no longer looked confused. They were glassy eyed, fixated on the Father-Son Duo as they approached slowly and deliberately.

"By order of Her Grace, Queen Venus, you two are hereby sentenced to death," announced the cop. He aimed his service pistol at the superheroes, as did the others. "And your sentence is to be carried out immediately."

Chapter 19

A flying superhero in red tights and a black mask fired bolts of plasma. Green spheres of concentrated superheated matter launched from his silver wrist launchers, but none hit their targets on the ground.

That didn't deter the angry mob of people from trying to take down those very same targets. They rushed toward them with knives, baseball bats, and their own fists.

All of Herald City was out to take down Blue Eagle and Switch.

"Careful!" yelled Blue Eagle as one of the plasma bolts nearly hit a civilian.

The Father-Son Duo were racing down a commercial street, trying to escape the mobs of people trying to kill them. Ordinary people with no powers chased them, some with household items like broomsticks and kitchen knives, and most unarmed.

They had stuck to the streets when the sky proved dangerous due to the flying superheroes that found them, but now it seemed like collateral damage and civilian casualties were on the table if it meant their deaths.

That, the frailty of the civilians, and Switch's vulnerability made for a very precarious situation.

Dashing through the streets was too dangerous for everyone around them, so Blue Eagle grabbed Switch under his arms and lifted him up into the air, flying toward the top of a multi-story parking garage a few buildings away.

"Let's take this fight away from civilians, shall we?" he said to both his sidekick and his pursuer.

They landed and turned as the red-clad superhero ascended above them, aiming his gauntlets at them.

The sound of metal scraping and wings flapping caught Blue Eagle's ears.

He whirled around to see a large bird-like creature flying toward them. He estimated her wingspan to be about twelve feet wide and her length to be about as long. Brown fur covered her body, including her bat-like wings. He and Switch locked eyes with her, the eyes of a lioness with brown hair.

She landed on the pavement. In a flash, the furry bird transformed into a snarling wolf. Despite the change in animal, the rough shape of a lioness's head remained, as if her very form couldn't decide whether she wanted a lioness or wolf face.

To their side, the sound of metal scraping across metal grew louder. A pair of titanium scorpion stingers appeared, piercing the aluminum siding of the garage. Another figure pulled himself up and squared up with them. He wore dark green armor over his entire body and a black visor over his eyes. The insignia of a scorpion glowed with a fierce green light on his chest. He raised his arms, menacingly displaying the stingers extended from his wrists.

"This is insane. How does everyone seem to know where we are?" growled Switch as their foes circled them, looking for a chance to strike.

"If each person is now one of Queen Venus's plants, then they all see what the others see," said Blue Eagle. "So long as one person sees us, the whole city sees us."

"Which means we're about to have company unless we can take these three out really fast," concluded Switch.

"Agreed," said Blue Eagle, firing his eyebeams at the red-clad superhero still floating above him. His attack was met with a sustained plasma bolt, the two blasts canceling each other out in a shockwave of heat and dust.

The scorpion stinger guy lunged at Switch. The teen sidekick dived out of the way just as the wolf girl pounced at him from behind, landing on the scorpion guy instead.

Blue Eagle took to the air, dodging plasma bolts that seemed to get closer to hitting him as he got closer to his opponent. He kept an eye on those gauntlets. With his durability, getting hit by a plasma bolt wouldn't be fatal, but it *would* be painful.

He skillfully maneuvered around the mindjacked superhero and grabbed the back of his collar. "Switch, you ready?" he called.

Switch held the wolf girl over his head with one hand. "Ready, Blue Eagle!" he confirmed as she struggled in his grip.

"Hey, you put me down so I can bite you!" she demanded, her voice signaling an age of about twelve or thirteen.

Blue Eagle and Switch hurled their respective catches at each other. The plasma bolt guy and the wolf girl collided in midair and fell unconscious to the pavement. The wolf girl's body reflexively transformed into its default form, a humanoid lioness superhero in pink sleeveless tights, with a short white cape and a lion's head insignia on her chest.

The scorpion guy leapt to his feet. "I will kill you both in the name of Queen Venus!" he bellowed, lunging toward the superheroes.

Blue Eagle and Switch effortlessly sidestepped him, each grabbing a wrist with one hand. He struggled, but could not escape the grip of hands that could bend steel. Not letting him go, the Father-Son Duo used their other fists to seemingly tap him lightly on his chest before releasing him.

They turned away as he stumbled around and slowly reached for his chest.

"Good job," said Blue Eagle to his sidekick as the scorpion guy sank to his knees.

"Thanks," said Switch as the scorpion guy slumped to the ground, unconscious. "Hopefully, we have a few minutes until the next wave comes."

Blue Eagle frowned, then started looking around. "Actually, I can hear them coming now."

The sound of footsteps surrounded them. From the level below, a mob of people rushed toward them angrily. They were just ordinary people; a man in a business suit, a young woman in a sweater, a deli shopkeeper with the stains of various foods still on his apron. But they weren't themselves. They had bludgeoning weapons of all kinds. If they weren't a danger to the superheroes, they certainly were to themselves.

From the other side of the garage, the stairwell door burst open. More of Herald City's citizenry rushed onto the scene, roaring as they charged at the heroes.

"More of them!" cried Switch. "What now?"

"Is your superstrength still working?" Blue Eagle quickly asked.

"Yeah!"

"Then follow my lead!" commanded Blue Eagle, raising a fist.

Together, the Father-Son Duo punched the ground beneath them. Their firsts were strong enough to turn pavement to powder.

The mob stopped as they saw Blue Eagle and Switch fall through the pavement. They shielded their faces as dust filled the air, obscuring everything in front of them. A series of crashes could be heard; the sound of two superheroes smashing through each level of the parking garage.

When the noise finally gave way to silence and the dust settled, there was a large hole that led to the ground level.

And no superheroes.

"I can't see them," said one woman, cautiously approaching the hole and looking down. Others followed suit, trying to get a glimpse of blue and white tights. "Not just down there. I can't *see* them at all."

"Everyone, careful! Step away from that hole! The floor ain't stable," cautioned a construction worker. He raised his monkey wrench. "We should get down there right now. Those two couldn't have gone too far!"

The crowd turned toward the exits, starting back downstairs with renewed vigor. No one noticed the brown sedan with two superhero passengers pull out of the garage.

Chapter 20

"Carla! Carla!" exclaimed Jasper happily as he rushed inside his apartment and closed the door behind him.

His wife rushed in from the other room. "Jasper? Honey, what's wrong?" she asked as he hung up his coat and took an envelope out of the pocket.

"Wrong? For once, absolutely nothing!" he cheered, leading her into the kitchen. He opened the envelope and dropped the contents on the table.

It was more cash than either of them had ever owned in their lives.

Carla's eyes widened in shock. "The job paid that well!?"

"It did. It had multiple parts, resulted in a massive victory for my boss, and," he took her in his arms and gently kissed her forehead, "I played a key role in its success."

"This is great!" beamed Carla. "Maybe we won't even have to use it to pay off our debts now that we are finally united under the rule of the glorious Queen Venus."

He gently pushed her away. "What did you say?" he whispered.

"Now that we are part of Queen Venus, perhaps the Charlemagne Family will forgive our debts," she elaborated.

And with that, Jasper felt everything fall apart around him. It was like being at the bottom of the ocean. He felt everything but his own body.

She frowned. "Strange. I can't feel you as part of the same tree," she remarked. "You weren't brought into the forest like we were?"

Jasper started to respond, but she glanced off to the side as if someone was there telling her something. She nodded in understanding.

"No, you weren't. Queen Venus needed people separate from her to operate the Treescraper's functions, or else it might be too much for her powers to handle," she realized. She sighed. "That's a shame, but I'm still proud of you."

She placed a hand on his shoulder. "You did what was needed for Rosa," she said, leaning in and kissing him.

He slowly nodded. "Is Rosa home from school yet?" he asked nervously.

"Yes, she is," replied Carla, perking up. "Actually, wait until you see what she did today." She turned to the hallway. "Rosa? Sweetie, come show Daddy what you made in school today."

His daughter ran in from her bedroom. "Daddy, Daddy!" she exclaimed happily as she leapt into his arms for a hug. "I'm glad you're home!"

"Of course, munchkin. I missed you," said Jasper.

For the first time in his life, that was a lie.

She turned a piece of construction paper she was holding toward him. His heart sank when she did. It was a crude crayon drawing, with four stick figures. There was one small one and one with a crown and no face, taller than the others. But he knew what these figures were.

"Look at what I made! It's you and me and Mommy and Queen Venus. She's protecting us," she said, pointing at each of the figures. "Isn't it great?"

Jasper clenched his jaw. "It's great, sweetie. It's great."

He could barely contain himself. He couldn't be here any longer. He felt sick.

"Alright, my little artist. I gotta go," he said, kissing his daughter on the forehead.

"Where are you going?" asked Carla as he stood up.

"I, uh, have some more things I gotta do at the Treescraper," he lied.

She smiled. "I'm so proud of you," she said. "If you're gonna be back late, I'll put your dinner in the fridge. Don't want your burger, chicken, and pork to go bad."

"Thanks," he whispered, stumbling awkwardly for the door. He fumbled for his coat. With one last glance toward his confused family, he left.

He started down the hall, but stopped almost immediately. Tossing his jacket to the floor, he slumped against the wall.

This couldn't be right. Carla. Rosa. His family, now two more of Queen Venus's puppets.

How could he allow that? How could he accept that?

His eyes narrowed with resolve. His lips pressed together. He grabbed his jacket and strode quickly to the stairwell.

He couldn't.

And he wouldn't.

Chapter 21

The car made a turn onto the quiet street in yet another deliberate attempt to avoid the main roads. People went about their day. Nobody noticed the costumed superheroes in the driver and passenger seats.

"So let me get this straight," started Blue Eagle.

"Yeah, I went through this bit with Jasper. Go ahead," said Switch.

"Queen Venus had been working right under everyone's noses to implant important people in the city's political, business, and scientific sphere with Planticites; tiny parasites of her own creation that, when implanted in a person, makes them essentially one of her plants, able to be controlled like the vines and roots she materializes from the ground," continued Blue Eagle.

"Or the monsters," said Switch. "But yeah, she developed that using her own chlorophyll blood and her innate knowledge of plants. Which is about normal for her," he added.

"But she wasn't powerful enough to create these Planticites en masse and infect the whole city in one go," continued Blue Eagle, focusing as best he could at driving casually and keeping people's eyes off them. It had been a while since he drove a car, given that he could fly anywhere he wanted. "She needed an enhancement."

"The Photosynthesis Enhancer from the Herald City BioGenetics Lab."

"She knew creating and deploying these things would require a massive structure, so she mindjacked Mayor Warren, the city parks commissioner, and the CEO of the construction company to push through the construction of a foundation at Liberty Park. Something they would never do because building a skyscraper there would be, frankly, a stupid idea."

"A *very* stupid idea," agreed Switch. "But yes."

"Blizz Kid and Poster Boy also got those Planticites stuck in their heads and have been working for her this whole time."

"For the most part. They were mainly distractions. Like, it didn't matter that Blizz Kid didn't steal the Photosynthesis Enhancer. The whole point of them being there was to implant the lead scientist. This way, if they failed to steal the machine, she would just give it to them anyway."

"And catching them was pointless because the Police Chief—"

"Who was also mindjacked."

"—was letting them out while they did big distraction heists, keeping us from catching wind of any of Queen Venus's activities," said Blue Eagle, a notable disdain in his voice over the undermining of their efforts to take down supervillains.

Switch nodded. "That's right."

"And we didn't notice anything until it was too late and there was a giant tree building in the middle of Liberty Park spitting out mind control parasites," concluded Blue Eagle.

Switch nodded. "That's a pretty definitive recap, yes."

There was a pause before Blue Eagle added, "And you knew about this this whole time and didn't say anything until it was too late."

Switch turned his attention outside, not saying anything.

"Why didn't you say anything?" asked Blue Eagle.

The only answer the teen was able to give was a slight shoulder shrug and a grunt.

"That wasn't a rhetorical question," said Blue Eagle tersely. "I want to know why you didn't tell me the moment you knew Queen Venus was up to something."

There was another pause. "I wanted to do this one on my own," said Switch softly, not looking away from the darkened streets outside his window.

"You've learned nothing since you started as my sidekick three years ago, then. You should know that Queen Venus isn't someone you can deal with on your own. What were you *thinking*?"

Switch groaned. "Can we not talk about this now?"

"We've been driving around for an hour, trying to avoid being seen by anyone and taking the least obvious routes to Liberty Park. And we have some time left. So now is the time to talk about this," said Blue Eagle. He glanced at Switch. "Why didn't you think to come to me once you found out what Queen Venus was up to?"

"Because...." started Switch. He took a breath. "Because you never would have believed me."

Blue Eagle shot him a bewildered glance. "What? Sure I would have," he insisted. "Why wouldn't I believe you? You're my sidekick."

"If you knew I had gotten the information from a henchman, what would you have said?" asked Switch.

"Information about a supervillain plot is always valuable."

Now it was Switch's turn to shoot the veteran hero a bewildered glance. "Really? Would you have believed that Jasper had a change of heart and wanted to help, or would you have said what you said earlier?"

"That's different. You were trying to hide this guy from the consequences of his actions."

"Yeah. I didn't want him to go to jail if he had truly changed and was trying to help. If I was trying to protect someone who was trying to help, someone who may not have come forward if he knew you'd just pop in and arrest him or whatever, do you think I'd have been able to tell you anything?"

Blue Eagle started to answer, but stopped. He frowned, focusing on the road as he turned a corner. Switch watched him, then turned back to the window.

"Sorry," the older hero eventually said. "For not immediately taking you on your word for your suspicions."

"That's okay," sighed Switch, still watching people go about their day in the darkened city. "I didn't really communicate them that well."

There was a moment of uncomfortable silence. Blue Eagle glanced a couple times at his son, his jaw tightening.

"Switch, I...." he started, taking a moment to find his words. "I know I'm hard on you sometimes, and I dressed you down pretty hard before. But I have decades of experience as a superhero. You're a kid with very little experience and unreliable powers.

That means you can't afford to make mistakes. Not in what we do."

He waited for a response, but Switch didn't react at all.

"All I wanted for you is to become a superhero on your own one day," continued Blue Eagle. "And that means becoming the sort of superhero that can be effective, not the type that trusts criminals that go on to betray them."

Switch felt his insides sting upon hearing that last part. Like it was a mistake that showed his inexperience, incompetence, and inadequacy. Like he wasn't good enough to wear the costume and be a superhero.

But there was one thing he had to know.

"Why.... After you knew I was getting information from a criminal, why were you still ready to go check out Liberty Park?" he asked.

"I may not trust a criminal," said Blue Eagle, giving Switch a supportive smile, "but that doesn't mean I shouldn't trust my own son."

Something lifted off Switch's shoulders, or so it felt. He gripped the edge of the seat to keep his mind off the emotion bubbling up inside him.

"Thanks, Dad," was all he could say.

Suddenly he wished he could go one-on-one with Queen Venus. He felt like he could take her on—or take on some of the even worse supervillains in other heroes' Rogues' Galleries—by himself.

They turned a corner. "We're here," announced Blue Eagle.

The car pulled into an empty parking lot. Multiple dirt paths at the other end led into Liberty Park, the massive urban park at the center of Herald City. Normally, there were events, a zoo, gardens and lakes, and grassy fields for ballplaying and dogs to run around in.

Instead, the massive tree that became the new city skyline took up most of the view in front of them, even though it was about half a mile away in the two mile long park.

"You ready to cut down this tree?" asked Blue Eagle with a grin as they approached the closest spot to one of the paths.

"Oh yeah!" said Switch, pounding his fist into the palm of his hand. "We've got the element of surprise on our side. The bad guys won't know what hit 'em!"

The car launched into the air.

Neither of them had expected it. The vehicle was suddenly thrown upward. It seemed to hover in place for what felt like ages in the air before eventually landing upside down in the grass just at the edge of the parking spaces. Windows shattered and the metal frame bent into something unrecognizable. The car alarm moaned pathetically as what remained lay on its roof, its exterior crushed to the point of there no longer being a viable interior.

Out of the pavement was a large chunk of ice, a boulder of frozen water ripped out of the ground and brought into existence.

Blue Eagle and Switch floated in the air, looking down at the wreckage.

"Looks like we got out just in time," remarked Switch.

"Shall we go confront our attackers?" suggested Blue Eagle.

The pair floated down gently to the grass, squaring up as they stood face to face with Poster Boy and Blizz Kid.

The ice villain laughed. "Almost had you that time," he said.

"Blizz Kid. Not surprised to see you out of prison. You made record time," said Blue Eagle.

"I had help."

"It's about time you two showed up," said Poster Boy, an asymmetrical smirk crossing his face. "Now the party can *really* get started."

"Sorry, we only deal with *real* supervillains," said Switch, folding his arms.

Anger flashed behind Blizz Kid's ski goggles. "'Real villains'. I'll show you how real...." his voice trailed off as Poster Boy placed a hand on his shoulder.

"Oh, Jackie Boy," said the other villain, stepping forward. His grin grew wider. "I'll make sure you get slashed to ribbons by a flock of *me* for that one."

"Yeah, that was cold. Like corpses," threatened Blizz Kid, his lips curled into a snarl.

Poster Boy's eyes lit up. "I know! I'll put up posters of the photos of our two favorite eagles, dead in their open caskets," he said, making a sweeping motion with his hand. "Picture perfect."

"Enough of this nonsense," said Blue Eagle. He looked around. "Queen Venus! Show yourself!"

Immediately, superheroes started appearing from everywhere, flying out of or from behind the Treescraper. Others ran or swung into the area. Some materialized into existence if their powers allowed.

Blue Eagle and Switch recognized some of them, such as the plasma bolt superhero or the shapeshifting animal girl, now back in her strange furry bird form. But there were more. A boy in armor with the TomorrowTech Industries logo. A man in a trench coat with blades for fingers. A hulking shark-human hybrid that leapt out of the ground as if it were water, the grass shimmering and swaying like waves before returning to normal. Other superheroes hovered in the air or stood ready on the ground, most of them low or mid tier heroes that Blue Eagle would have little trouble with one on one.

The sounds of sirens and approaching cars could be heard suddenly. Seven HCPD squad cars rolled up into the parking lot. The cops piled out of the vehicles and took cover behind them, drawing their weapons and aiming at the Father-Son Duo.

From the sides, recognizable gang members wearing solid but different colored shirts stepped into view, cocking their guns. A group of well dressed mobsters—low level members of the Charlemagne Family—readied their Tommy guns, the weapons complimenting their striped suits and old-style wool fedoras appropriately.

The eagle-insignia'd heroes were surrounded.

"This is not good," said Switch.

"No kidding," replied Blue Eagle.

At that moment, the ground began to shake.

Everyone nearby moved out of the way as a mass of vines sprouted from the grass. They parted and retracted, revealing Queen Venus.

"You asked," she said with a hint of majesty in her voice, gracefully gesturing to herself, "and here I am."

"Good of you to just show yourself," said Switch, punching the palm of his hand. "Saves us the trouble of having to bust into your Treescraper to find you."

"This is it, Queen Venus. Our rivalry ends here," declared Blue Eagle.

"I agree," said Queen Venus. She cocked her head to the side. "Tell me, would you like a lesson in, let's say, my personal botany?"

"No," replied Switch flatly.

"As you know, I have full control of plants. Not just the plants that come from my body, but all the flora in Herald City," she explained anyway. "I may have needed a boost for my Treescraper, I'll admit, but all plants in general are under my command. But do you know what my plants do when I'm not controlling them?"

"Hate you and plot your downfall?" said Switch dryly.

"They do nothing," she continued, ignoring his snide remarks. "They're just ordinary plants, until...."

She gave a graceful gesture toward some shrubbery a few yards away. It quivered and let loose a low, rumbling growl. She swept her hand toward the closest tree. A hollow slowly opened, wider and wider, jagged teeth of bark forming around its edges. The whole tree leaned forward with a quick jerk—branches and limbs moving as if flesh and blood—and let out a bellowing roar.

"....until I command them to be *more*," finished Queen Venus. "And if I am not directly controlling them, they are normal plants, engaging in their normal biological processes."

She waved her hand again, and the suddenly-sentient plant life went back to their normal non-carnivorous states. The tree pulled back, its gaping maw closed. It was as if it never moved.

With a click of his teeth, Switch jeeringly asked, "That's interesting, but what does that have to do with anything? Do you want to make us feel bad for stepping on the grass?"

"All the citizens of Herald City are now my plants," she reminded him. "And though they know to serve me, they act as they normally do until I exert direct control over them."

Switch frowned. "What are you hin—"

That was all he got out before his chest exploded with pain. He started to fly, which was strange because he never activated his flight. The world spun madly around him for what felt like the longest 1.78

seconds of his life before he felt the pain of his back hitting grass.

He started coughing as he fought to get air back in his lungs and bring his focus away from the pain radiating through his entire upper body. He curled into a fetal position, holding his chest and groaning in pain. He hadn't had any of his powers activated, so that attack hurt him far more than it normally would in a fight.

Whatever hit him, it had some level of superstrength. The blow wasn't enough to injure him, but it was enough to send him flying, and enough to *hurt*. He cursed his lack of constant invulnerability as much as he cursed the pain receptors in his sternum for holding his attention so strongly. He pushed through the pain and got to his knees, wondering what hand-shaped plant could have gotten the drop on him.

He looked up. His eyes widened. His skin turned pale. The pain disappeared, replaced by an all encompassing numbness.

"Oh no...."

Blue Eagle stood over him, his arm still raised from having effortlessly swatted Switch away.

"There is one plant I decided not to execute direct control over until this very moment," said Queen Venus. She cocked her head sideways, leaning slightly forward in reserved enjoyment. "Isn't that right, *Blue Eagle*?"

"Yes, Your Highness," answered Blue Eagle, moving to stand next to her, his dull eyes fixed on Switch.

Chapter 22

"How?" uttered Switch, wincing as he pulled himself to his feet. "How is this possible?"

"The leaves on top of the Treescraper are lenses so perfect that they can momentarily redirect the very beams of light they are carrying a Planticite in," explained Blue Eagle. His eyes locked onto Switch's. Somehow, despite their dullness, they still carried that sense of stern judgment that he often looked upon criminals with. "We thought we had gotten behind cover, but the tiny little creatures were redirected at the last second, hitting both of us in the backs of our necks."

Switch rubbed the back of his neck, a slow sense of understanding washing over him. "That moment.... We were being chased.... I had my invulnerability activated," he realized. "That protected me from getting mindjacked, didn't it?"

"It did."

The teen surveyed the situation. It was not good. There were dozens—no, over a hundred—superheroes and villains, cops, and criminals surrounding him. All had the same dullness in their eyes.

"So what now?" he asked defiantly, pushing down the fear bubbling up inside of him. "Is there a Planticite with my name on it?"

Queen Venus lightly snorted. "I have no use for another weed," she told him. She slowly turned her head to Blue Eagle. "Not when I have the flower I've always wanted for my garden."

The mindjacked hero's eyes narrowed. "Switch, if you really want to be a solo superhero," he said, menacingly approaching the teen, "now's your chance to prove you're ready."

"Wait," squeaked Switch. He put a hand out as he backed away. "Wait, Blue Eagle, stop."

"My son? A coward? What sort of sidekick are you?" admonished Blue Eagle coldly as he came closer and closer. "Face your death like a man."

The teen superhero raised a clenched fist. "I've activated my superstrength. You know I'm stronger than you with it on," he warned. The desperation in his voice did little to add teeth to his warning.

"Good. Let's test this!" boomed the older hero, lunging toward his son. A mighty fist connected with the boy's left cheek.

Switch stumbled back, the momentum nearly causing him to turn around completely. The blow didn't hurt that much; thanks to his superstrength, his body was durable enough to take what superpowered beings dished out. His chest hurt more from the movement than his face did from the punch itself.

He grounded himself and prepared a counter attack, but stopped.

He didn't want to fight his father.

Could he even win against his father?

The moment of hesitation cost him dearly. Blue Eagle scored an unprotected hit right into Switch's chest.

The young fighter let out a pained cry as he slumped to his knees, holding his aching torso.

Looking down at the teen, Blue Eagle gave a huff of frustration.

"Pathetic! Stop holding back, because I certainly am not," he demanded, thrusting his foot forward to stomp Switch in the skull. Switch caught his foot in time and shoved it away, causing the possessed man to stumble back a few steps.

Switch forced himself onto his feet to capitalize on Blue Eagle being off balance. He went for a punch, but an eyebeam blast to the chest sent him off his feet and flying back a few yards onto the concrete pavement of the parking lot.

"What, did you think we were just going to throw half-hearted fisticuffs?" asked Blue Eagle coldly, slowly approaching Switch, who struggled to collect his wits as he lay on the pavement.

A white boot that could crush the concrete it walked on roughly pinned Switch to the ground by his chest. He cried out in pain.

Blue Eagle's eyes glowed red.

"Ooh, this part should be fun," marveled Queen Venus, squirming as she rubbed her hands together gleefully. "I love violence against children."

"Dad....please. You don't have to do this," pleaded Switch, his face contorting in pain from the pressure on his chest. "You can fight this.... We can fight Queen Venus together!"

"Oh, Switch. Here you are, believing your enemies could be redeemed with an earnest talking to, maybe some free money thrown their way," said Blue Eagle coldly. His eyes widened, preparing to fire. "This is where I become the parent....of a dead child."

Switch shut his eyes.

The sound of tires screeching across pavement filled the air.

Everyone turned toward the sound of a car skidding into the lot. The cops dived out of the way as it blew past their cruisers.

Blue Eagle frowned, starting in the direction of the car. "What is—"

The car slammed into him at top speed before coming to a sudden stop. He was unprepared for the hit, and the force was powerful enough to send him sprawling to the ground twenty feet away.

The passenger door opened, revealing Jasper behind the wheel. "Get in, kid!" he beckoned, waving him forward.

Switch scrambled to his feet and dove into the empty seat next to Jasper, closing the door.

Slamming onto the gas pedal, Jasper turned the steering wheel as far to the left as it would go, making the tightest possible turn he could make. He leaned forward, his eyes focusing on the space between the police cars he came through. Holding his breath, he gunned it for the only exit they had.

A look of anger washed over Blue Eagle's face as he got to one knee. "You!" he snarled. His eyes glowed red. "I'll kill you both with....one...."

The glow disappeared from his eyes, which grew dull and lifeless. His body relaxed and slouched forward slightly as he got to his feet.

"Very good, Blue Eagle. You are as excellent a servant as you were formidable a foe," complimented Queen Venus, standing beside him. But there is no need to waste the time to pursue. The Blue Eaglet and that little man will never be able to do anything. Two confused birdies in my vast garden. My energy is better spent preparing the next batch of Planticites."

She turned and started back to the Treescraper.

"After all," she added, "Herald City is not the only garden I have to tend to."

Chapter 23

The car spiraled through the air, passing over three city blocks before landing in the West River. Water flooded inside through the broken windows and dislodged engine hood, and the whole thing sank like a stone.

Pleased with his throw, Switch stepped back through the gate beneath the on-ramp to an overpass. Its lock lay broken on the ground, having been effortlessly crushed into tiny pieces just moments ago.

"You know, we could have just hid *my car*. Not throw it into the West River for a touchdown," hissed Jasper with wide eyed incredulity and frustration, watching the feat of super athleticism from the darkness underneath the overpass.

"It's the only way to keep everyone off our trail," said Switch, shuffling past him. "Someone will eventually track the car down. Let them search the bottom of the bay for it."

The small-time crook clenched his teeth and shook his head. "Fine," he spat. "Now that we're without transportation or allies, what do we do?"

Switch slumped hard against the wall, sliding to the floor. "There is no next," he informed Jasper. His eyes rested on the dirt in front of him. "It's over."

There was a heavy pause before Jasper took a step forward. "Are you kidding me!? You're really gonna sit there while Queen Venus takes over the city?"

"Yes," replied Switch glumly. He glanced up at Jasper. "She *already* took over the city."

"So what? You superheroes always save the day in situations like this!"

"Us superheroes aren't usually henchmen of the main villain. She's got *everybody* on her side now. There's nothing I can do to stand against them."

"You really gonna tell me that after what I just did?" Squatting down, he jabbed a finger into Switch's chest. "I rushed into the fray to save your life! I did

236

that so that you could help me stand up to Queen Venus! Not just roll over and let her win!"

"I remember you lying to me about the subway bomb threat so you and your buddies could rob some charity thingy, and *that* being part of some big distraction so that me and Blue Eagle wouldn't notice her working in the shadows," snarled Switch, angrily shoving the finger away. He got to his feet, Jasper following suit.

"I remember you worked as a henchman for her in—what was it? Three jobs? Four? I forgot. And who knows how many others I don't know about, all a part of this?" he continued. "You want to accuse me of just allowing Queen Venus to just conquer the city, but you actively *assisted* her in all this. So I don't want to hear a word about rolling over when we've already lost. If there was still a Herald City to fight for, I would take you down right now for your crimes."

He roughly pushed past Jasper, standing next to the gate as he gazed absently across the darkened street. In anger, he pounded his fist against the gate.

"My dad was right. Someone like you is nothing but a criminal to your very core," he muttered.

Jasper opened his mouth, having an airtight defense against the mischaracterizations Switch uttered. He shut it, that defense suddenly not seeming so good. His mind thought up another strong counterargument against the teen's insults, but before he could utter it, it suddenly didn't seem so strong.

There was a long moment where no one said anything. The darkness and silence of the city said everything that needed to be said.

"Sorry," he finally said.

With a quiet huff, Switch waved his hand dismissively. "It doesn't matter," he said, not even bothering to look back. "There's no reason to fight now. Even Blue Eagle is under her control."

Sighing, Jasper sat against a metal trash bin in the corner. "My wife, Carla, and my little girl, Rosa, are under her control now, too."

There was a heavy pause. "Sorry," said Switch.

"I went back home for a bit and they seemed normal. Right until they started talking about the glory of Her Royal Highness and all that," continued Jasper quietly. "After everything I had done to protect them, *this* is what happened."

He picked up a bottle cap off the ground and absent-mindedly fiddled with it, deftly moving it between his fingers like a coin pickpocketed from an unsuspecting tourist.

"After we last spoke, I was 'napped by a mob enforcer. I think I told you earlier that I had bills and debts. I didn't mention that they were to the mob. I was threatened after we spoke. The loan shark gave me just three days to pay it back, or else they'd go after my wife. That's why I took the job, and lied about there being a bomb on the subway."

"It's okay. Sounds like you didn't have a choice."

"That's what I said once to Carla. But she had the right idea. I was blaming myself for my poor lot in life. And yeah, so much of it ain't my fault. But all I ever did was let the bad circumstances drive me around like a speeding car with no brakes. But the missus said something to me, that just because the world around you's forced you into a bad position doesn't mean you don't have a choice on what to do next. I didn't realize that until it was too late, but I ain't gonna whine about how it's all unfair and that there's nothing I can do."

He tossed the bottle cap against the wall and stood up.

"I'm making a choice to save my family, a choice that started with saving your life," he announced. "Even if I fail, even if all I do is get swatted away after charging in half-cocked like I was doin' before I found you out there, at least I'll have chosen to try."

The young sidekick turned around as Jasper placed a hand on his shoulder. "Whaddaya say, Mr. *Superhero*? With your dad part of her hive, what's your choice?" asked Jasper. "You gonna lay under a bridge and do nothing, or you gonna do whatever you can to save him and the city, even if you fail?"

Switch thought for a moment. There wasn't much to think about. "What did you have in mind?"

"You mean like a plan?" clarified Jasper. He shook his head. "Dunno. Didn't think it too far beyond burst into the Treescraper with a gun and take it to the ol' witch, if you get my drift."

"You said that Queen Venus was planning to hit other cities with those Planticites," said Switch, stroking his chin. "We gotta get in there, figure out a way to stop the production, and destroy this giant tree once and for all."

"The Treescraper is guarded by every superhero and supervillain in the city, along with cops and criminals, all serving as her eyes and ears," reminded Jasper. "We won't be able to just burst through the front door."

A thin smile crossed Switch's lips as an idea came to mind.

"Then we'll take a different approach," he said.

Chapter 24

A beam of light shined against a small section of the massive tree that loomed over Herald City. The grassy field before the massive structure that took up the square acreage of a city block began to shudder as the lights grew larger. Grass retracted into the dirt, creating a path for the truck to drive smoothly on, its headlights illuminating the side of the Treescraper..

A section of trunk opened up like a garage door, and the truck drove inside unimpeded. The "gate" shut behind it, and the grass regrew itself immediately.

In a wooden crate in the back of the cargo truck, Jasper whispered, "This was a terrible approach."

Both he and Switch were cramped inside the crate. They laid opposite of each other with their knees bent in order to fit. If it weren't for the lights from their cellphones, they would be unable to see each other or the dark blue jackets and jeans, baseball caps, and sunglasses they had changed into.

"This was a terrible approach and a terrible plan," he whined again. "Whose plan was this?"

"Yours, mostly. Remember?" said Switch. "I just said we needed to go stealth. You came up with this whole plan."

"Oh, right," said Jasper, resigned to his fate. "This is what happens when I make major life choices. I get to be stuck in a cramped little box with the only superhero in Herald City that isn't out to either mind control me or disintegrate me on sight. This is such a bad plan."

"Stop that. It's a great plan," admonished Switch. "Let's go over it one more time."

"Good idea. I could use the reminder."

"Our goal is to get inside the Treescraper and figure out how to, a) sever the connection between Queen Venus and everyone she's mindjacked, and, b) stop the production of any more Planticites. You told me that you saw a good chunk of this place when you were here before, so you know that it will take some time to produce enough Planticites to target another city, *and* that it takes a great deal of effort on her part to control everything and everyone."

"I was only up there for a little bit," clarified Jasper. "But yeah, I saw the important parts of that giant tree."

"So then, you remind me why we're cooped up in the back of this truck," urged Switch, nudging Jasper's leg.

"Ah, well, it's the only way in without being seen," recounted Jasper. "Despite what Queen Venus says, everyone under her control aren't literally plants. They're humans. And other assorted alien and magical beings that live in Herald City, sure. And they all need supplies in order to function and live. *And* those people are needed to operate and maintain the Treescraper, because it's all too large for Queen Venus to do so on her own, even with her powers. *And* the hallways are gonna be filled with superhumans, cops, crooks, and all will kill us on sight. So getting these disguises and hiding in the supply trucks are so that we can make it inside without being seen and get to the control room on the top floor."

"You said earlier that the control room has some weird biocontrols that she needed regular uninflected henchmen to operate because the Treescraper and all its functions are too much for her alone," reminded Switch. "That means if we can get up there and access those controls, we can put an end to all of this."

"Right. *If* we can get up there without being caught," said Jasper in a way that suggested he wasn't so sure they could do that.

"Hey, long shot plans like this are part of the hero business," said Switch. He flashed a comradely smile. "And, like it or not, Mr. Clemens, you're in the hero business now."

Jasper felt a knot tighten in his stomach. He wasn't sure if he had what it took to be a hero.

At the same time, he felt a flush of pride. He *never* thought he would ever actually be a hero.

They lurched suddenly as the truck stopped. The flush of pride Jasper felt evaporated, anxiousness and adrenaline kicking in. No more sitting in crates. They were in it now.

The muffled sounds of footsteps and conversation leaked into the crate. They could hear the sounds of heavy objects being moved.

"Sounds like someone's unloading the crates," noted Switch.

"What do we do?" whispered Jasper nervously. His wild eyes darted nervously around their wooden box despite there being nothing to see.

"*You* be quiet and let me do what I do," said Switch, pushing the crate open and disappearing into a motion blur of superspeed.

Shocked, Jasper scrambled to his feet. "What the—What the heck do you think you're...."

His voice trailed off as he saw Switch standing over the unconscious forms of three construction workers.

Looking back at him, Switch answered, "I'm doing what I do."

"I see," said Jasper, looking back and forth at the three men in shock. The teenager defeated three men much larger than him in the time it took Jasper to stand up.

"Hopefully, Queen Venus didn't notice three of her new hive mind henchmen getting knocked out. But just in case, let's hide the bodies," suggested Switch.

Jasper nodded in agreement. Together, they lifted the three men and hid them in one of the shipping crates.

"You know, I was gonna say something like 'Special Delivery'," mused Switch as they worked, "but it didn't feel right. These guys are workers, not henchmen."

"Thanks," said Jasper dryly. "But even if they were, would the lame one-liner really have been necessary?"

"No, but sometimes, if you wanna be a superhero, you have to lean into the whole thing," answered Switch unapologetically. They closed up the crate, and he patted Jasper on the shoulder. "If you wanna be a hero today, you'll have to do a one-liner or a pun when you win a fight against a bad guy."

"I'm not too good with that."

"Don't worry. You only have to do it once."

They cautiously approached the door that led out of the loading dock they were in. Beyond it was a hallway lit by electric lights. The occasional door was placed on either wall. People went in and out and about their business. No one seemed to notice the duo wearing sunglasses indoors.

"Keep your head down," advised Switch. "If one of them sees us and realizes who we are, *everyone* does."

For some time, they moved through the corridors and rooms of the Treescraper, never lingering in one place for too long. They were just two more people working for the glorious Queen Venus. Jasper's knowledge of the organic building was limited, but enough to keep them moving towards staircases and elevators.

They poked their heads into some of the rooms. While some seemed to serve a purpose—a supply room, a kitchen, a tool shop—others were just empty squares or rectangles of wooden tree trunk, illuminated by more lights.

"I can't believe there's all this stuff in a building that literally just sprang to life today," marveled Switch as they passed by working restrooms. "I mean, not ten minutes ago, we passed by a water purification room, and another room with backup generators. She really went all out with this one."

"There's actually quite a bit of cool stuff in here," said Jasper. "I got a bit of a tour during the short time I was here before I was paid and told I could go home, but they showed us where some of the stuff for living quarters will be. Apparently there will be dorms, a mess hall, a gym, a weapons room—"

"A *weapons* room? Seriously?" interrupted Switch.

Jasper nodded. "Shipments of guns will be moved in later so that everyone here who doesn't have superpowers will be able to help defend the Treescraper in case of an attack from the military or aliens."

"That makes sense," conceded Switch as they entered a stairwell. "You never know when interdimensional beings from an alternate negative Herald City will invade. They can smell vulnerability like a—*Bloodhound*!"

He yanked Jasper out of the stairwell and back into the hallway, hurriedly walking away from the stairs as fast as possible.

"What's wrong? What's going on?" whispered Jasper through his teeth, nervously looking behind them.

"I saw Bloodhound coming down the stairs," answered Switch, keeping up his quickened pace.

"Bloodhound?"

"Yeah. A superhero. Not a particularly nice superhero, though normally a superhero nonetheless. One of the grimdark ones."

"I figured from the name. What's his powers?"

"He can catch the scent of his enemies from a mile away and track them anywhere, so we need to get as far away from him as possible."

They rounded a corner....and nearly walked right into Clay and three henchmen.

"Hey! What are you.... *Clemens*!" shouted Clay.

The henchmen pulled out their guns and aimed at Jasper. The man held his hands out and ducked, acting entirely on fear and instinct.

Switch was in front of him before the gunshots sounded, tanking the blasts with his invulnerability. Bullets bounced off of him. Flattened shells landed harmlessly on the floor.

The henchmen looked at Switch. Switch looked at the henchmen. Clay looked at both sides, then turned and ran.

The henchmen rushed at Switch, trying to hit him with the butts of their guns. Like the bullets, the metal and plastic did absolutely nothing to him.

Switch didn't hesitate. He started throwing haymakers, hitting the three men with everything he had. Some of the blows connected, some were blocked, and some missed altogether. But he put all his might into each swing, seeking a knockout blow with every punch as the wild fight between the four bounced between one wall of the corridor and the other.

"Hey, Jasper, a little help here?" called Switch as one henchman landed a punch he didn't even feel. "These guys are stronger than me, and my invulnerability only lasts a couple of minutes."

"Oh...." said Jasper, realizing that Switch's invulnerability didn't mean he was strong enough to defeat the three men so easily. He got to his feet. "I got ya kid!"

"Everyone, leave Switch for later! Go after Clemens first!" suggested one of the henchmen.

"No. Keep the boy busy while *I* go after Clemens."

Everyone turned to the source of the low, growling voice.

The man stood at the end of the hall, back toward the stairwell. He wore a leather trench coat over a black jumpsuit. There were no gloves or boots. Instead, he had dark brown paws like a dog.

He glared at them, his face that of the angriest bloodhound dog anyone had ever seen.

Jasper's jaw dropped. "Oh, shoot. Is that–"

"Bloodhound," finished Switch.

The canine superhero slowly stalked forward, picking up speed as he eyed Jasper.

"This is trouble!" cried Switch. "Jasper, get out of here!"

Without hesitation or protest, Jasper turned and bolted past Switch and the henchmen. He turned the corner and ran down the hall.

Bloodhound broke into a run. He tore off his trench coat, revealing his jumpsuit in full. He leapt over the others and landed on all fours, not breaking stride as he chased after Jasper.

Chapter 25

The sound of his own breathing deafened his ears and his pulse pounded in his temples.

Jasper ignored all of that as he ran as fast as could through the corridors of the Treescraper. He took every corner he could, shoving aside anyone who tried to get in his way.

He looked behind him and immediately regretted it.

The humanoid dog-man superhero, Bloodhound, tore through corners, skidding to a stop and realigning himself with ferocious precision. Sometimes his momentum carried him with such force that he slammed into a wall while making a tight turn.

Every time Jasper looked back, those eyes—uncharacteristic of the hero's namesake—seemed to stare right through him. Almost *past* him, as if he weren't there.

"That is the angriest bloodhound I ever seen," lamented Jasper as he ran. "How can someone with that name run that fast?"

Bloodhound said nothing. His massive presence barreling through the hallways was his answer.

Making another right, Jasper suddenly found himself in a garden. There was a hard dirt path separating two rectangular fields of tall flowers ranging from three to four feet tall. At the end of the room, about fifty feet away, was the exit.

The scent from the flowers was overwhelming, and Jasper found himself holding back a series of coughs.

"Oh, this stuff's powerful," he choked, letting loose a cough. Holding his mouth over his nose, he leaned toward a flower to smell it. He immediately recoiled. "Powerful, and just what I need."

As quickly as he could, he removed his sunglasses and jacket. Putting the shades into his jacket pocket, he then plucked the flower and rubbed the petals and pistil all over the jacket.

The sounds of heavy footsteps grew rapidly closer. There was no time to waste.

He rushed to the other end of the garden and threw his jacket as far as he could down the hall, then immediately jumped into the flower bed and crouched in the midst of a group of four foot tall tulips.

"Track that, you stupid mutt," he hissed as he waited.

As if on cue, Bloodhound barreled into the room. He stood on two legs and began to sniff the air. With the face of a bloodhound contrasting against his sharp gray eyes and bared teeth, he looked like a grizzled veteran warrior seeking his final hunt.

Jasper did not want to be his hunt, final or otherwise.

Bloodhound shifted suddenly toward the other door, his nose pointing straight forward. He started moving quickly but cautiously across the garden.

This was exactly what Jasper wanted. Lure Bloodhound out the door with the jacket's scent, then sneak out and try to make his way back to Switch.

His heart thudded as the dog-man's gaze was focused dead ahead. The superhero sniffed the air, his ears up and alert.

The reformed criminal fought to slow his breaths. The fact that this thing was a *superhero* scared him. He knew that a situation like this was a risk every time he took a job, but seeing Bloodhound up close and hunting him made his blood curdle.

His heart leapt to his throat as the mindjacked superhero grew closer, now directly perpendicular to him.

Jasper was almost home free.

With a sharp movement, Bloodhound leapt into the flowers. Jasper cried out as he felt two rough paws grip the back of his shirt and hurl him across the room. He landed in the flowers, the dirt and plants dulling the impact of the landing.

It still hurt.

"Do you think I'm stupid?" growled Bloodhound, stalking Jasper. Bone claws protruded from his knuckles, two per hand. "I could smell you, even with all these flowers overloading my senses!"

"Why does a bloodhound-themed superhero have claws like that?" cried Jasper, his eyes widening at the sight of the sharp claws. They looked like they could easily tear through flesh. He scrambled to his feet, stumbling back as he did so. "I would expect that from someone dressed like, I dunno, a wolverine or somethin'!"

"You stink of fear and treason," insulted the superhero, his face cringing with contempt. He stared Jasper dead in the eye as his canine upper lip curled, revealing his fangs. "Let's dance, bud."

He rushed forward, ramming his shoulder square into Jasper's chest and wrapping his arms around him like a linebacker bursting from the scrimmage. He slammed Jasper against the wall, pinning him against the rough tree wood.

"Wait! Please, don't!" pleaded Jasper as Bloodhound pulled his fist back, ready to make the kill.

"Sorry, bud. But all enemies of Queen Venus must *die*."

Jasper grasped at Bloodhound's forearm, trying desperately to pull free. It was no use. Bloodhound didn't have enhanced strength, but he was still at peak human strength. Jasper wasn't.

"Please! Bloodhound, *no*!" he begged, his eyes meeting his killer's.

Except their eyes *didn't* meet. Bloodhound's eyes were sharply shaped, but they dully stared at his neck.

Despite his imminent death, a sudden realization hit Jasper all once. So many things came together.

The way Bloodhound slammed into corners or nearly missed turns.

The way Bloodhound never actually looked around when he was hunting Jasper.

The way Bloodhound seemed to stare *past* him.

"You're *blind*!?" realized Jasper.

"Huh?" reacted Bloodhound, his nose scrunching and his ears raising. At no point did his eyes focus anywhere else.

In one last desperate attempt to survive, Jasper lifted his legs and shifted his weight to the right. It wasn't enough to break free, but it wasn't intended to. His body slumped down, still held up by Bloodhound's forearm. He immediately felt pain in his neck and collarbone.

But it was enough for him to grab the nearest flower, pluck it, and shove it right into Bloodhound's nose, cupping it around the snout.

Bloodhound let out a curse obscured by a sudden coughing fit. He stumbled back, unable to stop the severe coughs and repeated sneezing. His eyes watered shut, and he held his chest with one hand while reaching out with his other hand as if trying to get his bearings in a pitch black room.

This was Jasper's chance. He quickly got his footing back, clasped his fists together, and smashed the back of Bloodhound's neck with all his might, sending the superhero to the dirt.

He kicked Bloodhound in the ribs. Then in the gut. Then in the back of the head. Again in the ribs. Again in the gut. Again and again and again.

Bloodhound reached out for a swipe with his claws, but Jasper quickly moved out of the way. He circled around the possessed hero, who pulled himself to his feet.

"Where are you, you—" started Bloodhound, interrupted by a sudden sneeze. He didn't look around, but his ears pricked up and he tried to sniff the air, only to hack up saliva. "I'm a superhero. I gut criminals like you all the time. And this time, I will do it for Queen Venus! I—"

He whirled around, facing the door they came in. "There you are!"

A red laser blast struck him in the chest, sending him onto his back, skidding across the dirt path and coming to a stop between the fields of flowers.

"I did *that* for Queen Venus," declared Switch, standing in the doorway with a contemptuous look on his face.

The red glow faded from his eyes as the smoke faded from Bloodhound's chest. The canine superhero was knocked out.

Switch glanced over at Jasper. "Are you okay?" he asked the shocked man.

Jasper looked down at Bloodhound's still form, then at Switch, his mouth agape the entire time. "I....I can't believe I survived that...." he breathed, holding his chest and allowing himself to breathe. He gave a short laugh as the adrenaline wore off.

"I know the feeling," said Switch. He waved him on, starting toward the exit opposite of them. "Now come on. We've gotta move. Queen Venus knows exactly where we are and will be sending more mindjacked superheroes after us."

"That's fine with me as long as they're not one of the crazies like this guy," said Jasper with a gesture toward Bloodhound, a newfound confidence in his voice. "I don't wanna see anymore superheroes with *Blood* in their name."

They stopped on seeing a figure in the doorway ahead of them. Their jaws slowly hung open and their hearts stopped.

A man who looked like he was in his late thirties stood blocking their path. He had harsh eyes and a strong jaw. More than that, he had a massive chest, partially displayed through his black tights which exposed his left arm, shoulder, and side of his chest.

Jasper pointed at the man, all his confidence gone in an instant. "That's..... Thats...."

"I know who that is," interrupted Switch, not taking his eyes off the man who, unbeknownst to him, was about to fatally stab a gang member in an alley when the city got mass mindjacked.

"That's *Bloodpayne*," finished Jasper, forcing the words out.

"I'm fully aware."

"They say he stalks the Cellar District, gutting any criminal he sees with a giant knife," recounted Jasper from the stories of his fellow thieves and henchmen.

From his belt—filled with smoke grenades and handcuffs—Bloodpayne slowly pulled out a machete. He never took his eyes off them.

"Yeah, he does that," said Switch with one part fear, one part surprise, and one part exasperation.

"So....how do we take down this guy?" wondered Jasper, only for Switch to give the best possible answer he could.

He grabbed Jasper's arm and pulled him in the other direction. They ran for their lives.

Knife in hand, Bloodpayne stalked toward them.

"We have to keep moving! Bloodpayne could be anywhere," Switch told Jasper as they made their way through the corridors.

"What do you mean by that?" asked Jasper, nervously glancing behind him. There was no one following.

"Bloodpayne's a master of stealth," Switch hastily explained as they turned a corner and stopped short. "And because he can do *that*."

They both watched—Jasper with his mouth agape—as crimson red liquid poured smoothly from a ceiling air vent ahead of them. As it hit the floor, the pool of metallic red fluid began to rise and take a humanoid shape.

"Other way!" shouted Switch as he pulled Jasper in the other direction.

Now reformed, Bloodpayne stalked after them.

"I can't believe I just saw a man turn into *blood*!" cried Jasper as they moved through the halls.

"I don't think it is," corrected Switch. "He once said it was something else.

"Oh, you've met this guy before?"

"Yeah, Blue Eagle and I have met him in the past," replied Switch dryly as they entered a large cafeteria, complete with wooden picnic tables. "Our last meeting was one heck of a battle."

There was another door ahead that led to the kitchen, judging by the diner-esque swing doors.

They sprinted towards it, only for a swarm of cops to burst out with their guns drawn.

"Freeze! Herald City Treescraper Police! Get on the ground and place your hands behind your head!"

Switch stopped, but he didn't get on the ground. His eyes glowed, and his eyebeams forced the police officers into cover.

"Keep going!" he ordered Jasper. "I'll keep these guys busy and catch up to you!"

Jasper didn't like the idea. What would he even do *if* he got up to the top of the Treescraper on his own? Defeat Queen Venus in hand-to-hand combat?

There was no time to protest. The cops were pinned down, unable to get a shot off as Switch took potshots at them with eyebeams that would surely be running out at any moment.

With the police pinned down behind the tables across the cafeteria, Jasper had a straight shot to the kitchen. If he remembered correctly, there should be a back entrance that led to a shaft that would eventually be made into a cargo elevator.

He ran for it. Despite his full sprint, he felt himself holding his breath as he passed the cops. But they didn't shoot him full of holes, and he managed to get safely to the kitchen as the sounds of eyebeams and shouting grew louder behind him.

He burst through the swinging doors to see maintenance workers installing appliances. People tightened screws and connected wiring for refrigerators, freezers, ovens, and sinks.

"Really? They got a whole kitchen set up this fast?" he said in disbelief.

The workers turned to him. Their dull eyes seemed to flash in anticipation and menace as they got to their feet. With tools in hand, they stalked toward him.

Jasper looked around. Spying a set of knives in their holder, he grabbed the closest one and held it out. "Stay back! All of ya!" he ordered, the quiver in his voice betraying his show of bravery. "Not another step!"

Suddenly, a strong white-gloved hand was on his shoulder, and a massive machete held at his throat.

"Careful with that knife. You might just cut yourself," came the snarling voice of Bloodpayne.

There was nothing Jasper could do. If he resisted in any way, his throat would be slit.

Without a word, he dropped the knife.

"Good," said Bloodpayne. "Let's go. Queen Venus wants to see you."

Switch fired the last of his eyebeams before his power gave out. There was a moment of silence as the cops realized he was done firing. They rushed out with guns drawn.

Putting his hands up and getting onto his knees, Switch watched as the cops surrounded him, shoving him to the ground and placing him in handcuffs as per standard arrest procedure.

Chapter 26

Through her mask, it was difficult for anyone to detect the joy Queen Venus felt as the police brought in the handcuffed Switch and Jasper. But it was there, and it was immense.

She glanced to the right of the wooden throne she sat on, the sturdy oak reaching twenty feet high, and allowed herself to drink in the sight of Blue Eagle once again. Her worst enemy, now her right hand man.

There were better, more powerful superheroes that she could have by her side. Any of the Defending Champions, the world's premier superhero team, would provide more protection against would-be assassins. But *this*....this was too perfect.

She took a moment to glance around the auditorium-sized throne room. Still a bit bare, but it would soon be decorated with devotional works of art portraying her as a saintly savior and protector. This grand hall at the top of her Treescraper was far better than her old lair.

Off to the side were Blizz Kid and Poster Boy, a mere two of her loyal servants. She had no need for them specifically, but they had done so well in their parts to create all this that she decided to keep them close.

Beneath her mask, a smile formed. Cruel and malicious. She settled into her throne, crossing her legs and feeling the smooth wooden armrests. Switch and Jasper were now before her. The son of her archnemesis, and the traitor.

This was going to be fun.

"It's about time you got here," she purred. "If you wanted an audience with me, you should have just knocked on the front door."

Her captives said nothing. They wore stony expressions and kept their eyes downcast.

"Do you like my Treescraper?" she asked in a deceptively friendly tone. She made a sweeping gesture with her hand. "It took a lot of time and effort to build, but it was done more quickly and efficiently than any government effort. Score one for the private sector."

"More like the criminal underworld," grumbled Switch.

"What? You don't like this natural wonder towering over that sterile eyesore of a city?"

A pause. Switch looked up at her with a defiant eye. "I hope it gets burned down in a wildfire."

"That's no way to speak of the creations of your queen." She paused for a beat. "Kneel," she commanded.

Jasper immediately complied, sinking to his knees. He kept his jaw firm and his eyes downcast. But Switch stood tall. He looked Queen Venus right in the part of her mask where her eyes would be.

"Sir, I'm going to need you to kneel," ordered the police officer standing behind him.

"Bite me," growled Switch.

The cop immediately backed up and reached for his belt. "Suspect is not cooperative! Using non-lethal force!"

Pulling out his stun gun, he fired the wired bolt into Switch's back.

The boy screamed as hundreds of volts of electricity coursed through him. He sank to his knees.

"I'd say something....about America's police brutality problem," panted Switch as the cop deactivated the weapon and pulled the dart from his back, "but you guys are under her control so this time doesn't count."

"Ooh, a little anti-authority streak, I see. That's not the Switch I know," teased Queen Venus cruelly. "What has Blue Eagle been teaching you?"

"I thought I had been teaching you right, but apparently not," scolded Blue Eagle. He crossed his arms. "I never taught you to have an attitude like that to Her Majesty Queen Venus."

For possibly the first time in his life, Switch cast a defiant eye toward his father. "You taught me to stand up to thugs like her."

"Such hurtful words," remarked Queen Venus, theatrically placing a hand on her heart. "If I were a thug, I could have Mr. America fly right in here like a bullet and turn you into paste. I could have Lady Liberty slice you into ribbons, or Move-On drag you by the ankles around the world in an instant, or Nightlight burn you alive. I have the Defending Champions under my control. I have the Might Mutants under my control. I have the Terrific Ten under my control. I have *all* the superheroes under my control, and many of them are floating around outside this structure standing guard. I let you two go before because focusing my attention on you would have been too much of a waste of time considering all I have to do. But here you are so now I have to deal with you."

"So why bring us here?" pressed Switch. "Why not just sic any of them on us and be done with it?"

"I would if it were any other hero, but having Switch the Blue Eaglet helpless before me is just too *perfect*," she answered.

She glanced between the two eagle-themed heroes and scratched her chin.

"We have such a history, the three of us. The two of you, the Father-Son Duo, against I, the Noblewoman of nature, the Sovereign of the Forests and the Trees, the Empress of the Earth and all that which mankind destroyed," she said almost whimsically.

"Oh. So it's this, as always," groaned Switch, rolling his eyes.

"'This as always'," she echoed derisively. She leaned forward. "And yes, I *will* be the champion of a planet torn apart by climate change and industrialization. Humanity can't keep themselves from destroying the only world they have, so I will restore the natural order of things by having nature dominate man rather than vice versa. Every city on Earth will have their skyline dominated by my Gaian superstructure. Their people will be my plants. And this time, you won't be able to stop me."

A grin spread across Switch's face. "You say that every time! And every time, we stop you!"

Queen Venus paused, then gave a short laugh. "Uncuff them, then leave us," she ordered the officers.

They did as ordered, uncuffing their prisoners and leaving. The one uncuffing Switch smacked him upside the head before leaving. The teen grumbled under his breath as he rubbed his head.

"So what's up? You planning to kill me in a fair fight?" he spat, turning a sharp eye back toward her.

"Try as many times as you want. You'll never succeed!"

Queen Venus let out a throaty chuckle. "You're right. I won't succeed in killing you in a fair fight, because it won't be *me* who does it."

Slowly, with a cold and menacing deliberation, Blue Eagle started forward.

Switch's face dropped. He and Jasper stepped back as the possessed superhero stalked toward them.

"This is bad," said Jasper, his voice quivering. He glanced at Switch. "You think you can beat him?"

"Beat him? I can't even fight him," protested Switch.

"Kid, you're gonna have to do something, 'cause your old man's gonna kill us!"

Before anything else could be said, Blue Eagle pushed off the ground, rearing his fist back as he rocketed toward his sidekick.

Jasper stumbled back as he moved out of the way. He saw Switch looking like a deer in headlights and was not about to be the same bloody smear that the boy was about to be.

A fist that could shatter a building made contact with flesh and bone.

There was a loud burst—like a thunderclap but with the sickening sound of flesh meeting flesh. It made Jasper flinch.

Switch planted his feet as he skidded backwards, his father moving with him. His outstretched hand still held Blue Eagle's fist, his superstrength activated just in time to allow him to catch the punch safely.

Despite knowing that both of them were superheroes and having lived in Herald City his whole life, Jasper felt his jaw drop watching the combined feats of strength. Blue Eagle's punch had enough force to send Switch skidding backward a full thirty feet, and yet the young hero held strong.

Watching them stand there—Blue Eagle still hovering in the air with his fist outstretched, and Switch with his heels dug in and knees bent after catching the punch—was surreal. It was like a splash page in a comic book.

"You've always been strong. Stronger than me," said Blue Eagle, looking Switch dead in the eye. "Do you think that will make up for your other weaknesses?"

"I won't fight you," said Switch through gritted teeth.

"Then you will die."

Another punch from Blue Eagle connected with Switch's cheek. The slender teen was thrown from his feet from the force of the blow, landing on his back about ten feet away.

Blue Eagle floated to the ground as he watched Switch pull himself back up.

"That punch would have killed a normal human, but your strength protected you," he said as his son got back on his feet. His eyes glowed red. "But will it still keep you alive after the next few minutes?"

Switch leapt into the air to avoid the eyebeams, his strength propelling him almost thirty feet up in the high throne room. But there was nothing he could do to dodge Blue Eagle's flying tackle. The wind was knocked out of his lungs as Blue Eagle slammed him hard into the wall.

"Because *I* will still be able to use all the powers I have at my fingertips," proclaimed Blue Eagle.

He tossed Switch to the ground.

"And *you* won't even be able to use the one power you have activated!" he admonished as Switch hit the ground hard, rolling to a stop as he laid face down on the rough wood.

Blue Eagle floated to the ground just as Switch was pulling himself onto his knees.

"*Fight!*" he shouted, angrily kicking the boy back down. "Don't just take it! Fight!"

Queen Venus leaned forward in her throne, rapt with attention. Blizz Kid's eyes were wide with glee, and he fidgeted in anticipation like a child. Poster Boy could barely contain his snickering every time Switch took a blow, and didn't even bother to conceal his ear-to-ear grin.

They were all focused on the battle so much that none of them were paying any attention to Jasper at all.

And the exit was right behind him.

He could get to safety before the villains tore him apart.

Blue Eagle watched as his son slowly pulled himself to his knees. "You only have minutes before your powers are gone," he admonished. "And once they are, you will die."

Switch looked up at his father. "Please, I don't want to fight you," he pleaded, putting his hand out.

There was no reasoning with him. Blue Eagle grabbed him by the collar and shouted, "I knew it! You're as weak mentally as you are physically!"

Switch winced. Even knowing that his father was mindjacked, his words stung. It didn't feel like one of Queen Venus's tricks.

It felt like they were coming from Blue Eagle himself.

"You became skittish lately. Caring more about the fantasy of rehabilitating those who commit crimes," continued Blue Eagle. He brought his face closer to Switch's, his lips curling into an uncharacteristic sneer. "Do you think you can rehabilitate *me*?"

He only got the quivering breaths of his former sidekick as a response. He slapped the terrified teen across the face.

"Well? Do you!?" he shouted directly in Switch's face. The boy squeezed his eyes shut. "Do you think you can *rehabilitate* me, just as you think you can make a law-abiding citizen out of....Clemens?"

He started to point in the general direction that Jasper had been earlier, but then stopped and looked around. Everyone did.

Jasper was gone.

A victorious smile spread across Blue Eagle's face. "Look at that," he pointed out. "Clemens ditched you. Left you to die. Nothing but a selfish criminal who will never change."

"Eh, I didn't even notice he was gone," commented Queen Venus. She shrugged. "No matter. I'll deal with him later. I just want to see the end of this fight."

"Do you see now?" continued Blue Eagle, coldly taunting his son. "Criminals like him, guilty of rebelling against Her Majesty Queen Venus, will never change. Not without a Planticite, but neither of you are worthy. You are weak in mind, and powerless physically. A superhero with powers that shut off? You will never be a real superhero, you will never be strong, you will never be anything but a worthless screwup sidekick, nothing but worthless trash."

"And you *talk too much!*" shouted Switch in anger, punching Blue Eagle with all his might square in the jaw.

The veteran superhero sailed across the room, landing on the uneven wooden floor and bouncing a couple of times before coming to a stop.

"Oh, come on!" cried Blizz Kid in anger, throwing up his hands. Poster Boy just scoffed and shook his head.

Queen Venus cocked her head sideways. "I know I'm rooting for Blue Eagle," she remarked, "but I still can't help but enjoy seeing that."

"You want a fight? Fine! I'll get you one, *Dad*!" snarled Switch, his lips curled up as he watched his father pull himself up. "We just started this fight. I still have time!"

Rubbing his jaw, Blue Eagle got back onto his feet. "Time? What, two minutes? Maybe three, if you're lucky? You think you'll be able to beat me in that amount of time?"

"I don't know. But I am *sick* of hearing you tell me how awful I am," said Switch. He opened his jacket and pulled open his shirt, revealing his costume underneath. "Now I'll show you what Switch, the *superhero*, can do!"

Chapter 27

The well dressed mobster patrolled one of the mazelike corridors of the upper floor of the Treescraper. He kept his Tommy gun at the ready.

Formerly a Charlemagne Family guard, he now worked for Queen Venus, as did every other human, alien, and interdimensional being in Herald City. He knew instinctively that he was to be on the lookout for Jasper Clemens because Queen Venus willed for everyone to be on the lookout for Jasper Clemens. And he instinctively knew Jasper was skulking around up there, because Queen Venus knew he was skulking around up there.

Keeping his eyes open, he allowed himself to get lost in the Blue Eagle vs Switch fight. Even though he wasn't there to see it, he knew exactly what was going on minute by minute because Queen Venus (and Blue Eagle, Poster Boy, and Blizz Kid) could see it.

What he didn't see as he walked past a corridor to his left was the punch that hit his temple with enough force to knock him unconscious.

Jasper shook his throbbing hand. He knelt down and picked up the submachine gun.

"I hope I don't have to use this. I ain't ever killed a man before," he said quietly to no one in particular. He looked around, and then nodded in the direction the mafia goon had been coming from. "I hope I can make it in time and that there's a way to break Queen Venus's hold on everyone. Otherwise, poor Switch is gonna be done in by his own dad."

Blue Eagle and Switch exchanged blows fueled by their superhuman strength. Both heroes—identically dressed in their iconic blue tights—went punch for punch as three of their villains looked on. Blizz Kid hooted and hollered while Poster Boy shouted advice to Switch meant to throw him off.

Queen Venus just sat comfortably on her wooden throne, enjoying her enemies going at it.

Blue Eagle and Switch had been her worst enemies since she started as a villain three years ago. She'd climbed the ranks in the Herald City villain hierarchy in record time, but the two of them always held her back. Now, under her control, Blue Eagle was going to kill Switch.

Once it was done, she figured she'd let Blue Eagle regain his agency so he could grieve over what had happened. A smile formed beneath her mask at the mental image of him cradling his son's dead body.

She should have thought of the Planticites *years* ago.

Under the weight of his son's punches, Blue Eagle began to falter. A haymaker sent the possessed superhero ungracefully stumbling back, but he quickly caught his footing.

"Not bad. You always were physically stronger than me when you used your superstrength," he remarked with what seemed to be a hint of pride in his voice. He rubbed his cheek. "Seems to be the universe's way of making up for the fact that you can only use your strength for five minutes. At most, if you're lucky. So if you *are* lucky, how much time do you have left? A minute and a half? Two, tops."

"That's about right," said Switch, his eyes narrowed fiercely. He raised his fists. "So let's not waste any time."

"Agreed," said Blue Eagle. He also took a fighting stance. "No more holding back. Let me take this to the next level."

In the biocontrol room, one the large burly bodyguards of Mickey, the Charlemagne Family loan shark, stood near a trio of henchmen sitting next to the many tree hollows that lined the wall. The room was mostly empty; it took very few personnel to run things. But Queen Venus kept protection up there just in case.

The curly red haired enforcer's eyes went from milky white back to their natural color. "Queen Venus wants you to let some light into the throne room," he told the smaller man closest to a hollow. "It's for Blue Eagle."

"Roger," said the non-mindjacked henchman. He gave a nervous glance to the other two crooks, who averted their eyes and backed away.

They were glad to be spared the Planticites, but being stuck in a room with a massive Charlemagne Family goon directly controlled by a very impatient supervillain meant their mental freedom was on borrowed time.

They had pistols, sure, but he had a bulletproof vest.

Without question, the henchman stuck his hands into the tree hollows.

Vines wrapped around his arms, reaching up and connecting to his temples. His eyes went white as he felt himself become the Treescraper itself.

From there, he executed Queen Venus's commands.

Hidden from their sight behind the entrance to the biocontrol room was Jasper, who had heard everything.

He gripped his Tommy gun tightly and hoped there was a chance he would be able to hold Rosa in his arms one last time.

In the throne room, cavities opened up in the wall ranging anywhere from the size of a small fist to that of a basketball. All led outside, where the branches of the Treescraper shifted and moved so that the leaves were in position. Sunlight was strategically channeled through the leaves and cavities, focused with pinpoint accuracy.

The beams illuminated Blue Eagle like a figure in a religious painting.

"Uh, what's going on?" asked Switch, raising a confused eyebrow. For all the light that was shining on the older superhero, it didn't seem like it was actually *doing* anything.

"Oh, you sweet, uneducated child," said Queen Venus with a throaty chuckle. "Blue Eagle is a plant."

Switch cocked his head sideways. "What do you me—"

He was cut off as Blue Eagle pushed off the ground and flew toward him, moving far faster than usual. Switch brought up his hands just in time to block, knowing his superstrength should allow him to easily tank the hit.

Instead, he felt an explosion of pain as his father punched him so hard that he rocketed across the room, slamming into the wall and leaving a Switch-shaped dent in it. He slid limply to the floor, the living wooden wall repairing itself as he did so.

He just barely got to his feet when he saw Blue Eagle standing over him, having crossed the room far quicker than he should have. Before he could even open his mouth to comment, Blue Eagle grabbed him and threw him into the air. The mindjacked superhero shot up into the air fast enough to catch up to Switch, slamming the teen into the ground with a double overhand smash.

"Plants gain energy and nutrients from the sun," explained Queen Venus as Switch fought to stand back up. "The Planticite has made Blue Eagle one of my plants."

Switch was already back on his feet as Blue Eagle landed, and he let loose with a thunderous haymaker to the jaw that sent his father stumbling back and almost sinking to his knees.

Almost. He spun around, his nose scrunched and his jaw tightened. He let out a single loud huff.

"So, well, I'm sure you can put two and two together," concluded Queen Venus as Blue Eagle again punched Switch across the room.

Again, Switch got to his feet. He wiped his mouth with the back of his gloved hand as he kept his eye on the slowly advancing Blue Eagle.

"Not much time left," he muttered. He quickly took a fighting stance, his cape sweeping behind him due to his snap movement. "I have to end this fight *now*!"

Bursting into the biocontrol room, Jasper opened fire on the Charlemagne Family enforcer.

The giant man had stood in his kitchen, in front of his *family*, while Mickey had implicitly threatened all of them.

The giant man, if given the order, would harm Rosa. His little girl. Until today, he'd been on standby to do just that.

Jasper aimed for the center of mass. Aimed to kill the giant man.

The henchman at the biocontrols cursed and ducked, the vines still attached to him. The other two took cover behind the other entrance, drawing their pistols.

The enforcer stumbled back a little, but stayed on his feet. He instinctively inspected his body armor.

Taking advantage of that distraction, Jasper closed the distance between them and rammed the butt of the Tommy gun into his forehead with all his might.

He felt a rush of power—and some pride—watching the large man slump to the ground, unconscious.

He aimed his submachine gun at the two armed henchmen hidden behind the wooden doorframe. "You think you got the firepower to take me down, boys?" he shouted.

The pair glanced at each other and shook their heads.

One suddenly slumped to the floor after a loud thud. The other followed suit.

"Wimps," came the voice of Clay. He walked past them into the biocontrol room, holding his magnum revolver by the barrel and tapping the butt into the palm of his hand.

"Clay," muttered Jasper. He gritted his teeth and pointed his SMG at him.

Clay scoffed. "Please. You're out of ammo," he said, casually pointing his gun at Jasper.

"You sure?" challenged Jasper.

"I heard that last burst. The click at the end. You heard it too. You're out of ammo. Now, put the gun down."

Jasper's face scrunched. He knew Clay was right. He did hear the clicks of the gun going empty.

With an angry huff, he tossed the gun away and slowly put his hands up.

"It's a shame," said Clay. "You've done such good work over the years. It's a shame you couldn't see the better world that was being created. The better world you could have lived in."

"Better!?" uttered Jasper in disbelief. "How is it better to have everyone in the world as some kind of mind controlled slave with a parasite in their heads?"

"Isn't it obvious? None of us wanted the risks that come with a life of crime, only the rewards. Now we've finally got that! The whole city serves us through Queen Venus. Anything we want is ours for the taking. Didn't you do all this to provide a better life for your family?"

"I did," whispered Jasper, frowning. "But a better life for them isn't being Queen Venus's drones. Carla and Rosa, I want them back!"

"Having a woman who's obedient might just have been what you needed," suggested Clay with a disconcerting grin.

Jasper looked him dead in the eye and said, "If that's the only way you can keep a woman, then that's a *you* problem."

Clay bristled at that. "This conversation's over, Clemens," he growled, aiming the magnum at Jasper's head.

The sound of someone entering the biocontrol room caught their attention, and they turned to see Mickey walk in, a faux charming smile on his face and a pistol in his hand.

"Seems like no one else is needed up here," he remarked, looking around. Jasper and Clay were the only two conscious people in the room. The henchman plugged into the hollows had already run away.

He looked away for a second, his eyes going milky white. They reverted to normal, and he turned back to Jasper and Clay. "The rest of the Treescraper is standing down. No more need to hunt down this delinquent deadbeat."

"I was just about to off him," reported Clay.

"You may want to hold for a moment," suggested Mickey. "We don't know if Queen Venus wants him dead or alive."

"Don't you know what Queen Venus wants? You're part of her, aren't you?"

Mickey chuckled. "She ain't paying attention right now," he said. "She's watching something *far* more important.

Queen Venus was literally sitting on the edge of her seat, watching the two superheroes battle to the death.

Switch unleashed a trio of powerful punches, each one hitting Blue Eagle square in the chest and causing the super man to stumble back. The teen went for a haymaker, but Blue Eagle stepped aside, grabbing Switch's cape and slamming him over his head to the ground.

"Oh, *finally*! About time the old man landed a nice hit like that!" fumed Blizz Kid, throwing his hands up in the air.

Blue Eagle reached down and grabbed Switch's cape again, throwing the boy away. Switch rolled to a stop and got back on his feet immediately, rushing toward his father and hitting him with everything he had in the jaw.

This time, it wasn't Blue Eagle that stumbled back in pain, but Switch. He let out a long, silent gasp and clutched his knuckles. It felt like hitting a brick wall.

"It looks like you're in cooldown right now," said Blue Eagle with a shrug. He advanced toward Switch, who timidly backed away. "That felt like the longest five minutes ever. But that's fine, because I'm going to make your last minute on Earth feel like a lifetime."

Chapter 28

Screams echoed through the throne room. Cries of pain bounced off the cavernous walls.

Despite his struggles, Switch could not break free of his father's bear hug. Feeling his spine and ribs being crushed in Blue Eagle's unbreakable grip, he threw back his head and cried out again.

He had only just been put in the bear hug, but without his superstrength, the pain was so incredible that it felt like an eternity.

If his powers took any longer than a minute to come back, he might not last.

"What's wrong? Too old for a hug from your old man?" taunted Blue Eagle, tightening his grip again to another chorus of screams. "There's been such a rift between us lately. So here, let me show you some *love!*"

A particularly painful crush elicited a high pitched scream.

"Please, let go! I can't breathe! Let go!" shouted Switch, his face contorted with pain.

"Blue Eagle making Switch beg for his life?" remarked Queen Venus. "No matter what happens, I will always treasure this moment."

A gurgling sound escaped Switch's lips. "Dad, please. I can't breathe...." he choked. "Please, you win. I give up, you win! Now let me go!"

Blue Eagle let out a frustrated huff. "I *told* you you weren't cut out for this. You only survived this long because I was watching you like a hawk, or an eagle, this whole time," he growled. "You thought you were ready to go out and be a superhero on your own? Well, this is the *result*!"

He squeezed Switch again, crushing the teen with his might. Switch screamed again, his voice shrill and scared.

Queen Venus watched with glee as Switch's screaming faded, his head threatening to limply fall back.

Switch needed his cooldown to end so he could use his powers to escape. It only took one to two minutes for them to come back, but it felt like he was being crushed for hours.

Only two minutes maximum was the amount of time he needed to hold out.

It had been less than a minute.

He felt his consciousness fading away.

"This guy's a traitor. I'm about to do him in," asserted Clay as he pressed the muzzle of his revolver against Jasper's forehead.

Jasper winced at the feeling of the metal being driven into his skull.

Mickey shrugged. "Queen Venus hasn't decided what to do with him, so I guess it's up to you what you want to do with this delinquent." He glanced at Jasper.

Clay thought for a moment. With a nod, he moved to put his gun back in his pants before instead striking Jasper across the face with it.

"I ain't gonna kill you, Clemens," he declared, this time actually putting his gun away. "I'm gonna beat the snot outta you until you don't want to live anymore. *Then* I'm gonna kill you."

Jasper barely heard him, the pain in his nose and mouth was so raw. But he did feel Clay's fist slam into his gut. A backhand across the face sent him to the floor.

Mickey laughed as he watched Clay hover over Jasper. "That's what he deserves for not paying his debts to the Family. Get a few extra licks in for that!"

Despite the homicidal criminal looming over him, those words grabbed Jasper's attention.

Debts? Family? These weren't the words of a mindless slave of Queen Venus. These were the words of a Charlemagne Family loan shark.

What was it that Queen Venus had said earlier about plants? That all plants were normal plants when she wasn't exerting direct control over them.

The real Mickey was still in there!

And, like it or not, the loan shark was the only person who could save him.

"Mickey," he called out desperately. "I *do* have the money to pay you back in full, but you'll never see a dime if I die."

Clay kicked him in the ribs. "Shut your mouth, Clemens! Think, why would he care about your debts at this stage of the game? The whole world is going to be part of Queen Venus! You think she needs the cash?"

Jasper ignored him, keeping his focus on Mickey. "Don't you work for the Charlemagne Family? Won't your boss be unhappy if you ain't collecting debts?" he pressed.

"The boss is under Queen Venus. We're *all* united under Queen Venus," said Mickey.

"I said shut up!" shouted Clay, reaching down and grabbing Jasper by the collar. He reared back his fist.

"Queen Venus doesn't control everybody all the time!" said Jasper frantically. "Life will be mostly normal, which means the Family will need money just like everyone else, which means collecting debts owed! And you can't collect from me if he kills me!"

Clay punched Jasper across the face, causing the man to momentarily go limp. "Looks like the

Charlemagnes are gonna have to write off that loss," he said. "Not that I care. You're dead, Clemens."

"No," said Mickey, holding out his hand. A slow realization washed over him. "He stays alive until that debt is paid."

"I don't care about your debt. I care about doing this little punk in," said Clay. He reared his fist back again.

Mickey's fist slammed into his face. Clay tumbled to the side.

"What are you doing!?" he yelled.

"You defy me, you defy Queen Venus," said Mickey.

Clay's nose scrunched and his lips curled. "Oh really?" he fumed. He lunged at Mickey. "Defy this!"

He tackled the loan shark to the ground. The two of them threw wild punches as they went down.

Jasper didn't even wait to see who would come out on top. He scrambled to his feet and rushed towards the nearest of the control hollows. It was unmanned; the henchman that had been there earlier must have slipped out during the commotion. With a quick but deep breath, he plunged his arms inside.

He ignored the deep-seated urge to remove his hands when he felt the smooth tendrils wrap around his arms. He winced as he felt the tips connect to his temples. His eyes went pure white.

Then suddenly, he had more than two hands, more than two eyes, more than two ears.

He had the whole Treescraper at his fingertips. Everything inside, he could see and hear as if he were personally standing in any of the rooms. He saw the various people wandering the halls, sitting down and resting, moving equipment, having conversations. He heard them all as one cacophony of voices, and then heard the distinct conversations that he focused on.

Strange. He thought being connected to the Treescraper would be like one strange trip that expanded his mind and made him feel like some sort of god. But no, he felt normal. It was like watching a wall of TV monitors and deciding which ones to focus on and which ones not to.

He could see inside the throne room. It wasn't good. Blue Eagle was crushing Switch in a bear hug, and Switch was on the verge of passing out. Queen Venus was enjoying every minute of it, Blizz Kid was yelling at Switch to die already, and Poster Boy was telling

"Jackie Boy" that there was no shame in "just letting go".

He could feel the Planticites in production, each one craving sunlight for energy. He could sense the energy being produced by every single one in every single mindjacked body. But it was strange. Blue Eagle's was running higher than the others. His Planticite was in overdrive.

There were cavities open in the throne room. Focused sunlight shined in, illuminating Blue Eagle from behind. Jasper raised his eyebrows, suddenly aware of what was going on.

"Little bugger must be full," he whispered knowingly. A sly grin crossed his face. "I gotcha, kid."

He willed the cavities to all close, save for one. He willed the leaves of the Treescraper to refocus themselves, aiming the sunlight in a single narrow, focused beam right at Blue Eagle's neck.

Even from where he was, he could still hear Blue Eagle cry out in pain. Could still see him release Switch, see him grab the back of his neck and stumble away. Could hear Queen Venus demand to know what was going on.

He could see the groggy Switch grimace as he pulled himself to his feet and grabbed his father's head, holding him so the ray of light stayed focused on the back of his neck.

He could even see the tiny Planticite crawl out of the back of Blue Eagle's neck–its body small enough to go completely unnoticed by even the superhero itself–before dying and turning to ash.

Despite his control over the Treescraper, Queen Venus's furious scream still unnerved him.

But that didn't stop him from feeling triumph and accomplishment as Blue Eagle and Switch slumped the floor, panting heavily.

"Yes! One down, an entire city to go," whispered Jasper dryly. His eyes lit up. "Wait! I have control of this whole thing! I can just *do* that for the whole city!"

He shut his eyes and concentrated. He suddenly became aware of all of Herald City. The roots of the Treescraper were deep and vast. He couldn't feel any of the people, but he *could* feel the Planticites. It would have been hard to explain the sensation to someone. It was like being near a hot stove, except being hyper aware of each particle of heat.

He willed the Treescraper's leaves and branches to reorient themselves. Cavities formed all throughout the trunk of the organic structure, making it look like it got hollowed out by termites. Or was turning into a giant piece of Swiss cheese.

When everything aligned, narrowed beams of sunlight showered the city like a dazzling light show. From afar, it looked like the leaves were rapid-firing laser blasts randomly over every part of the city.

But they weren't random. People all over gasped and grabbed the backs of their necks as they felt a minor burning sensation.

Ordinary people, superhumans, and everything in between cried out as the burning suddenly became intense. Almost everyone tried to move, but no one could escape the light. Even people inside buildings saw the rays bounce off walls and objects in seemingly impossible ways to hit the backs of their necks.

But it didn't last. After only a moment, it was over.

The shapeshifting lioness superhero in her pink tights and white cape rubbed the back of her neck, giving a wide, toothy grin as she understood what happened. Her tail wagged wildly.

The plasma bolt-firing hero in the red tights let out a quiet grunt and nodded.

In their separate locations across the city, Night Girl, Bionic Boy, and The Cheetah From Charon rubbed the back of their necks, wincing at the raw feeling on the back of their necks. Bionic Boy smirked. "Well, it's about time."

The Chief of Police sat dumbfounded at his desk. He moved the ice pack he held against his head to his neck, then winced and moved it back to his head.

The rays of light that pierced the Treescraper eventually faded away. Cops, crooks, mobsters, superhumans, and workers all throughout stood in confusion as they realized what was going on.

In the Clemens apartment, Carla held the crying Rosa, assuring her that everything was okay and that they were safe now. The heroes saved them.

And, with that, the citywide light show ended. The Treescraper's structure fixed itself, the cavities all closing.

Jasper smiled, knowing that the population of Herald City was free of the Planticites.

They were free of Queen Venus's control.

A sudden realization hit him.

He just saved Herald City.

Queen Venus stood at her throne, watching everything she worked for unraveling before her.

Her greatest plan yet to take Herald City for herself. To be its top super criminal. To remake the world into one of nature. To destroy Blue Eagle and Switch once and for all.

To *destroy Blue Eagle and Switch* once and for all.

Ruined.

Blizz Kid and Poster Boy sluggishly looked around, wincing as they rubbed the back of their necks.

"I'm not sure I want to be under Queen Venus's boot heel anymore," said Blizz Kid.

"Are you kidding? I would kill her for what she did," said Poster Boy, keeping his voice low. "Except I'm not suicidal."

Switch started to come to, his head feeling light and his back hurting like heck. He was snapped back to reality by the sight of his father slowly crawling toward him.

"Switch, are you...." started Blue Eagle, reaching toward his son. His voice trailed off when he saw his reaction.

Switch recoiled from him.

Blue Eagle's shoulders slumped. "Switch, it's me," he said in as quiet and calming a voice he could. "I.... I'm *me* again."

There was a moment that it seemed Switch didn't trust him. Finally, he sighed and his body loosened.

"Are you alright?" asked Blue Eagle, his voice apologetic.

"I.... I think so," breathed Switch. He looked around. "What's going on?"

A smile crept across Blue Eagle's lips. "I think your friend might have come through after all."

Switch didn't say anything. His eyes cast off to the side. He was waiting for the backhanded compliment or scathing criticism.

"Hey," said Blue Eagle, placing a comforting hand on Switch's shoulder. "You did good."

There was a silence before Switch finally said, "Thanks." During that time, he felt like a weight had been lifted off his shoulders. His heart raced, but not in a way that made him feel stressed.

They were words he hadn't heard in far too long.

The moment was interrupted when the room began to shudder. Everyone looked around in confusion as the shaking intensified.

"What's going on?" wondered Switch as chips of wood and handfuls of dust began to fall from the ceiling.

"I think that should do it," said Jasper, removing his arms from the control hollows. "That Photosynthesis Enhancer supercharges everything the Treescraper does, and I just set it to redline. Ain't no one here to shut it off, and Queenie ain't got the power to hold this thing together herself. This place is gonna be coming down soon."

He turned to see Clay standing over Mickey, who lay on the floor holding his nose. Coming up behind the hardened criminal, Jasper tapped him on the shoulder, punching him as hard as he could in the face when he turned.

"Consider that my final payment," he spat as Clay's body hit the floor.

Clay just laid on his side, not moving. Mickey groaned in pain, but didn't do anything either.

"You two stay right there for a minute. I gotta make an announcement," said Jasper, stepping over the two of them and walking toward a small table in the corner that had an old style radio transmitter. He had seen it earlier during his initial tour through the Treescraper and had learned that speakers were already being installed at the time so anyone in the biocontrol room could make announcements. He wasn't sure why such a thing would be necessary when everyone was supposed to be part of a hive mind connected to Queen Venus, but he didn't question it. It was conveniently available, and that was all that mattered at this point.

He clicked the transmitter on and spoke.

"Attention everyone! The Treescraper's about to come down 'round our ears in probably about ten minutes, given the rate of things. I suggest everyone get outta here before then! The paths to the elevators are open, and I left some windows open for those of you who can

fly. Any superhumans out there who can pull people out, please do so!"

The sound of a click indicated that the broadcast ended. Another shudder rocked the throne room as Blue Eagle turned toward Switch, who beamed brightly.

"Jasper ended up being a hero after all," the teen said proudly.

"Well, we can't let him take all the glory for saving the day," said Blue Eagle, his face turning stern. He faced Queen Venus. "I think it's time to bring a certain plant-conjuring supervillain to justice."

Switch stood next to his father. "Time to pluck this weed!"

Queen Venus stood in silence at the seat of her throne, glaring intensely at her two greatest enemies. Even her mask could not hide the quiet fury that bubbled up within her.

"Fortune has smiled upon the Father-Son Duo yet again," she fumed. She raised her head, looking down her nose at them. "But this isn't over. And mark my words, you *will* pay for this indignity!"

The throne began to lower into the floor, along with a few yards surrounding it. It was an elevator platform that quickly descended down. She glared at them as the elevator descended rapidly, never losing her footing for an instant.

As soon as her head was below the floor level, the hard tree wood closed back up.

A slight shudder rocked the room. "Looks like she escaped again," groaned Switch.

Blue Eagle's eyes narrowed. "I'm going after her," he declared. He glanced back at his sidekick. "Get out of here!"

The room shook again, this time more violently. It was enough to nearly make them lose their footing.

"I don't think that's such a good idea," warned Switch.

"It's probably not. Now get going!" ordered Blue Eagle as he flew up into the air. Looping backwards, he flew straight down toward the spot where the throne had been. He slammed into it like a meteorite, tearing through the floor as if it were made of paper and flying headlong into the dark depths below.

"Good luck," whispered Switch. He turned to leave—

—only for a thick beam of arctic blue and white to hit the doorway. A thick block of ice completely blocked his only exit.

"You're not going anywhere, Switch," said Blizz Kid chillingly. The remains of a frosty mist wafted from his fingertips. Behind him, Poster Boy sneered as he began hanging a poster on the far wall. "We're settling our beef with you *now*."

Blue Eagle continued his descent, plunging down the elevator shaft like a missile. It felt like forever.

His eyes were narrowed. His jaw tightened. He was determined to bring Queen Venus to justice.

The Treescraper towered over even the largest skyscrapers. Who knew how close he was to the bottom?

It didn't matter. He wasn't going to let Queen Venus get away this time. Not *this* time.

His determined look transformed into one of anger. He gritted his teeth. His eyes narrowed into furious slits.

And then they began to glow red.

Like a demon on the hunt, the red eyed titan continued down toward his prey.

Chapter 29

Beneath the Treescraper was a large subterranean room. Its walls and ceiling were different from those above it. Strong roots made up its surroundings, coming from a focal point above and extending and intertwining outward, puncturing and disappearing into the hard dirt below.

The section of ceiling right where the roots met burst open. A wooden elevator platform and throne crashed into the ground, kicking up dirt everywhere.

Queen Venus stumbled out of the dirt cloud, adjusting her thorned crown as she did so. Behind her, a pair of red eyes glowed ominously in the cloud.

"You seem awfully cranky right now," she said dismissively, wiping some loose soil off her costume.

She turned around. "Are your tights on a little too tight?"

Blue Eagle floated from the cloud, his eyes still a scorching crimson. He wasn't wearing the stern expression he had when facing down a criminal.

He was *angry*.

"You almost made me kill my son," he told her. There was a hint of a quiver in his voice, and a lot of fury.

She let out a loud laugh. "I know! That was my favorite part of this whole day!" She shrugged. "And, really, would anyone have really missed the boy?"

"*You almost made me kill my son!*" repeated Blue Eagle, shouting this time.

"I'll have to try harder next time."

"There won't be a next time. I'm bringing you to justice once and for all."

The room shuddered. Dirt and rock quivered beneath their feet. A smaller root dropped from the ceiling.

"And how do you plan to do that?" asked Queen Venus. She slowly raised her arms, gesturing around them. "This place is coming down around us, and I can escape through the ground while you won't have enough time to get out if you don't move now."

She removed her hooded cloak and folded it. "Of course, if you *truly* desire a fight to the bitter end," she said, placing it gently on the ground, "I'll gladly die for a chance to take you with me."

The red glow disappeared from Blue Eagle's eyes. "Who *are* you?" he asked as she placed her thorned crown on her cloak.

With a heavy glare, she coldly answered, "I'm the woman who won't fail the next time I try to kill your son."

The room shook violently. Large chunks of root fell from the ceiling. One root that was buried in the dirt twisted almost to the point of breaking.

Blue Eagle fired his eyebeams. Queen Venus sprouted vines from her shoulder blades which fired streams of acid.

The ice beam narrowly missed Switch as he kept near the ceiling. He expertly weaved around the arctic attack as it tracked him from below. Just a few feet above him, the ceiling was being inadvertently coated with a thick sheet of ice.

"Don't you guys wanna get out of here before this place comes down around us?" he asked, flying around and easily dodging the ice beam. "I'll be honest, I'm a little sore from my previous fight and would rather do this another day. If that's alright with you guys, of course," he added jestfully.

"This ain't gonna be a fight!" countered Blizz Kid hotly, his hand extended up toward Switch as he fired the continuous stream of ice at him. "It's going to be your execution!"

"I wish I had a dollar for every time a villain says something like that," sighed Switch. "All that cockiness, and the good guys still always win!"

As Blizz Kid let out an angry cry that Switch then mockingly imitated, Poster Boy finished taping the last corner of his poster. "Keep thinking that," he whispered. A grin spread across his face. "I've been saving *this* poster for a special occasion."

Blizz Kid fired another continuous ice stream from his other hand. The two beams collided, and it took Switch a second to realize that a second sheet of ice was being formed beneath him.

"Trying to trap me, huh?" noted Switch as the ice sheet was extending past him, leaving only a few feet between it and the ceiling. It was going to be like being trapped in an attic, except the floor was just ice.

He pushed off the ice repeatedly like an ice skater as he raced toward the rapidly closing hole ahead of him. He had to get out now if he didn't want to be trapped up there while the Treescraper was falling down around his ears.

Another shake. This one was far more violent than any that had come before. Switch skidded to a stop as he saw a chunk of tree wood shake loose.

Blizz Kid dived out of the way as a hundred pound piece of solid tree trunk crashed through the ice above and nearly landed on him.

"I think that's a sign that we can leave now," said Switch, floating to the floor. "We can finish this outside if you guys want, but I think we're all past the part where the good guys won and are celebrating our victory."

"I don't think so, Blue Eaglet," came Poster Boy's voice in a sing-songy taunt. "This isn't a superhero story."

"You know, I'd really prefer to be called Switch," said the superhero as he turned around. His eyes widened. "Oh no," he whispered.

Poster Boy stared down Switch with a slasher smile. Right behind him was a movie poster. *Grim Iron IV*. Dominating the poster was a muscular football player whose helmet had a metal mask that covered his entire face. In his hands were two rusty machetes. Next to the football player was the tagline, "Jackson Vermont is back! And he's gonna give you more than an Extra Point!"

"This is a horror movie," said Poster Boy as the homicidal athlete stepped out of the poster and into the three dimensional world.

Jackson began fidgeting his feet, like a linebacker about to charge.

"In the last film, Jackson was revealed to be unkillable before racking up the highest body count ever in a slasher movie," said Poster Boy. "You think you can survive?"

The horror movie villain charged.

Unlike every character to have had their sights set on by the movie killer, Switch did not scream. He did not run for his life up a flight of stairs. He did not even flinch.

Instead, he floated straight up into the air just in time.

Jackson passed harmlessly beneath Switch. Blizz Kid was now in his path. The ice villain brought up a thick sheet of ice between himself and Jackson just in time. The blades plunged through the sheet, the tips emerging from the other side and stopping just inches short of Blizz Kid's face, eliciting a very unsupervillain-like scream.

"Normally, horror movie villains don't go up against superheroes," laughed Switch, hovering a few feet in the air. "They usually go up against thirty year old actors playing teenagers without super*powers*—*!*"

He cried out as he felt himself fall out of the air, landing on his chest and stomach. The wind got knocked out of him, and he coughed as air reentered his lungs.

Poster Boy laughed. "At least you aren't being played by a thirty year old actor, Jackie Boy!"

Switch lifted his head to see Jackson taking a three-point football stance, ready to charge again.

Far behind him, Blizz Kid placed a hand on the ice that was blocking the exit.

Jackson charged at Switch.

"Uh oh!" cried the teen, scrambling to his feet. Without his powers, he was no match for a slasher movie villain.

He backed up, giving himself more time to react to the full sprint charge.

Jackson barreled toward him like an angry bull.

Switch bent his knees, ready to move.

When Jackson was only a yard and a half away, Switch dived to the side. The slasher villain ran past the hero—

"Oh—Wait! *Wait!*" cried Poster Boy, holding his hands out in front of him.

—and shoulder tacked Poster Boy, crushing the teen villain's body against the wall.

Poster Boy slumped to the floor, landing unconscious facedown. With him knocked out, Jackson vanished, reappearing in the poster as just a harmless movie advertisement.

Switch pulled himself to his feet, eying Poster Boy to make sure he didn't get back up. Taking a second to let him get his bearings, he whirled around, ready to take down Blizz Kid.

No one was there. The ice blocking the door had melted, reduced to a puddle of water in front of the exit. Two wobbly, weak pillars of ice stood on each side of the door. The middle had all but disappeared to make a path out.

"Looks like Blizz Kid escaped," muttered Switch. He turned toward the unconscious Poster Boy and shrugged. "Taking down one of them is pretty good, all things considered. For how much of a pain villain team ups are, I'll take it."

The Treescraper shook again, causing him to stumble. This time, the shaking did not subside. It became more and more violent.

He picked up Poster Boy and hoisted him over his shoulder. "Time to go!"

Shadows danced all across Herald City like a macabre puppet show from the heavens as the entire Treescraper shook. People rushed into nearby buildings as tree branches the size of 18 wheelers fell from the sky. Superheroes pulled people out of the way and caught falling branches before they could hurt anyone.

People fled the Treescraper as wood and dust began to fall everywhere. From cavities in the middle and upper sections of the structure, superheroes flew out holding those who couldn't make it to an exit on their own. A man made of black metal rode out on a slide that extended from his own feet, dozens of civilians riding down with him to safety. The shapeshifting lioness flew into a cavity and flew out with six terrified people clinging to her back. A section of ground shimmered as if completely liquid, and a shark-man hybrid hero leapt out, two people clinging desperately to his neck.

A pinkish-red chain wrapped around a branch, and Bionic Boy swung out. The superhero clad in red armor carried two unconscious people wrapped in another chain behind him. Landing safely near the crowd surrounding the Treescraper, he gestured with his arm, causing the chains to disappear.

The bodies of Clay and Mickey dropped unceremoniously to the ground next to his feet, both still out cold.

In the crowd, Jasper saw the two men. He was disappointed that they were alive but grateful that they were knocked out and in a public place. He wouldn't be threatened by them here. Clay was definitely going to jail.

"Jasper!" came a voice behind him.

He turned around to see Switch jogging up to him. There was a bright smile on the teen's face.

"I supposed we all have you to thank for saving the day?" said Switch.

Jasper gave a knowing smile. "I didn't have a choice," he said. He looked around. "Where's your dad?"

"He went after Queen Venus," replied Switch. A look of worry washed over him. "He didn't make it out?"

"I ain't seen him."

Before Switch could say anything, the Treescraper lilted. Its main structure cracked and tore apart, the weight of the lower sections unable to bear the weight of the upper ones.

"*Dad!*" he screamed as the Treescraper collapsed. He instinctively moved to run toward it, but Jasper held him back.

The sound of the wooden skyscraper imploding was deafening. A few of the superheroes in the crowd that had sound manipulation powers used them to damper it. The rest worked to protect the crowd from the falling branches and oncoming wall of dust. Shields, force fields, black holes, and other defensive powers protected them while all manner of laser beams and energy blasts destroyed the falling debris.

It was minutes before the dust finally settled, helped on by multiple superheroes with wind and weather powers. The sound of destruction hung in the air like physical debris.

And the whole time, Switch never took his eyes off the Treescraper. Or, rather, the big pile of firewood that used to be the Treescraper.

It felt like there was a long silence. There wasn't. Some people cheered while others murmured in shock that it was over. Other people asked if they saw this or that person. But Switch didn't hear any of it. All he could do was stare at the rubble of the massive tree, desperately hoping to see some movement.

There was no way Blue Eagle could still be in there. He *had* to have gotten out. He was *Blue Eagle*, after all!

His eye caught movement. A piece of wood being pushed aside. From the rubble emerged a middle aged man in ripped blue tights. The outfit had holes in the chest, shoulders, and knees. Dust and soot stained the white cape. The man staggered toward them, very much tired but very much alive.

"*Dad!*" he shouted again, this time in triumph and relief.

Blue Eagle was alive.

Cheers erupted from the crowd as the beloved superhero lifted off the ground, tiredly floating over to his sidekick.

"You made it!" exclaimed Switch. His face slowly dropped when he saw the look in Blue Eagle's eyes.

Exhaustion. Frustration. Apathy.

"Are you alright?" asked Switch, his forehead wrinkling with worry.

Blue Eagle just sighed and nodded.

"What happened to Queen Venus?" asked Switch. His shoulders slumped. "Did she escape again?"

Blue Eagle nodded again. "I don't think she'll be bothering us for a very long time though," he told Switch.

The way he said that made Switch apprehensive. Normally, they were words that should have him rejoicing. The longer they all went without seeing or hearing from Queen Venus, the better. In fact, he was pretty sure they've both said that exact phrase at one point or another after defeating her over the years.

But the way Blue Eagle said it wasn't confident or triumphant or relieved.

It was *regretful*.

"What *happened* down there?" he asked his father.

"Nothing for you to worry about," replied Blue Eagle, walking away from Switch.

With a sudden determination, almost anger, the superhero approached Jasper. With a stern glare, he grabbed the confused and startled man by the arm.

"Hey, what are you–?"

"I'm aware, Jasper Clemens, that you are, in part, responsible for everything that's happened," said Blue Eagle, holding firmly. There was no way Jasper was escaping his iron grip. "I'm turning you over to the police. You'll answer for what you did."

"No! Blue Eagle—Dad! You've got it all wrong," pleaded Switch. "Jasper saved everybody—including me, from you. He's the one who freed everyone from Queen Venus's control and stopped her from unleashing the Planticites on the world. He is the hero of this whole thing, not us or any of the other superheroes. He's not a criminal anymore. He's a changed man!"

"No, he's not," countered Blue Eagle, steely, yet empty inside. "He's a criminal. And he's going to pay for his crimes."

He didn't say another word. No one did as he dragged Jasper toward the nearest group of police officers, leaving Switch to stand there helplessly and watch.

How could such a triumph evaporate in an instant? He thought his father learned that people could change.

What happened?

Chapter 30

It was a beautiful day. The sun shined brightly and there wasn't a cloud in the sky. It was so clear out that one didn't even need super-vision to make out the distinctive features of Mareplane as they galloped through the air.

Construction and repair crews were already working to rebuild the damage caused by the falling tree branches, and logging companies were finishing up removing the last of the wood.

It had only been four days, but that was just how things were in Herald City. Supervillains attacked and caused damage, superheroes stopped them, and the city put things right.

That's why the crowd was gathered in front of City Hall. That's why Mayor Michael Warren was thanking everyone for returning to normalcy so quickly after such a particularly devastating attack. And that's why he was granting Blue Eagle and Switch the key to the city; for delivering a blow to Queen Venus so decisive that it would be a long time before she struck again, if at all.

Switch smiled for the cameras as they posed with the mayor, who was handing them the ceremonial key. It was a mostly put-on smile; it wasn't the first time they were granted this honor. Plus, he couldn't stop thinking about Queen Venus. Or Jasper Clemens.

Was she really gone? If so, for good? What made Blue Eagle so sure? And what would happen the next time she returned, if there was a next time? How long would their "peace" be (peace being quite relative as far worse supervillains for far bigger superheroes were still out there)?

And Jasper? Could he convince his father to use his influence to ask for clemency for Jasper, whose trial would be starting tomorrow? For the DA to drop its charges, or for him to testify to how Jasper saved the day, or to request a lighter sentence in light of his heroism? He was certain someone would listen to a superhero as influential and popular as Blue Eagle. Why was he being so unreasonable again?

Warren moved out of the way so the reporters could get pictures of Blue Eagle and Switch holding the key together. While Switch held the practiced smile his father had him doing for the press since he was twelve, he noticed that Blue Eagle was looking unusually serious.

"What's wrong? Smile. We saved the day again and are getting the key to the city," he said under his breath.

"I'd smile more if you'd gotten a haircut before this event," said Blue Eagle.

It was a fight for Switch to keep the smile plastered on, and he felt it grow wider and less natural. He instinctively ran a hand through his hair, the bangs reaching all the way to his eyebrows.

He buried his emotions and his growing love of longer, messier hairstyles like in anime, and continued to smile for the cameras.

"We, the jury, find the defendant guilty, Your Honor."

Switch felt his insides wrench as the jury rendered their verdict.

The trial had been quick. The very picture of a speedy trial, in fact. It only lasted a couple of hours, and the jury deliberation was just over fifteen minutes.

It wasn't much of a trial. The evidence was overwhelming. It really came down to whether or not the jury was moved by the later acts of heroism, and their guilty verdict said if all.

The judge banged his gavel. "May the defendant rise."

Jasper, clad in his orange prison jumpsuit, rose alongside the public defender.

"Jasper Clemens, you have been found guilty of aiding and abetting a criminal conspiracy to destroy public property, commit acts of theft, assault with a deadly weapon, mind control all of Herald City, and insurrection against the municipal government of Herald City," informed the judge. "Your sentencing will be next week. In the meantime, you will remain in the care of the Herald City Department of Prisons. Court is adjourned for the day."

With another bang of the gavel, the trial was over.

Sitting in the front row of the gallery, Switch heard a cry next to him. Carla Clemens had lost her last shred of hope that her husband would be coming home. Now, without him, she was wondering how she would care for their daughter, who she had to bring to the trial with her because she couldn't afford a babysitter.

"Don't worry, man. I'll figure something out," Switch assured Jasper as the bailiffs led him past the bench. "I'll speak to the judge about a lighter penalty or to find out how to request a pardon or something. I dunno, but I'll do something. You don't deserve this. This isn't fair."

Jasper stopped in front of Switch. "Don't bother. I used to say the same thing. And it is true," he said. He gave Switch a faint smile. "But I recently learned from a young superhero that you're still responsible for your choices even when it seems like you haven't really made any at all."

He looked at Carla, still sitting with her head down, tears rolling down her cheeks. Rosa sat next to her, confused. At six years old, she couldn't understand the ramifications of what was happening.

"At least I know I made the right choice when the time came," he added. "At least I can feel some self-respect for the first time in my life."

That was all there was to say. The bailiffs nudged Jasper toward the door in the back corner that would lead him to the holding cells, and then his transport to prison.

Everyone began to file out. The judge had already entered his chambers. Carla picked up Rosa and left silently. She didn't even thank Switch for the offer to help her husband. That would have required some hope that there was something he could do, and she didn't feel that.

Switch didn't either.

As he watched the courtroom empty out, he marveled at how he could feel so defeated after such a decisive victory.

David Dufraine sat in his office in the insurance brokerage, going over paperwork. He leaned back in his chair, unable to concentrate on the client file in front of him.

A faraway look came across his face as he allowed his gaze to settle on a random spot on the wall. He felt distant from everything. Forlorn. He still wasn't over the shock of his final battle with Queen Venus. He still didn't know how he could ever tell Jack.

If he could ever tell Jack.

He decided then and there that the boy would never know the truth. *No one* would ever know. Let the truth die, and let the rubble of the Treescraper be its grave.

A knock on the door startled him out of his thoughts. "Come in," he called, getting to his feet.

The door opened, and in walked David's appointment.

"Good to see you! And thank you so much for coming back," said David, walking to the door and greeting the man with a professional smile and a firm handshake. "I'm sorry I had to skip out on you last time."

"No worries," assured the client. He nodded toward the shelf against the side wall. "After all, saving the world comes first, doesn't it?"

David allowed his gaze to follow the client's. On the shelf, there was a new framed newspaper clipping he'd just put up yesterday.

"*TIMBER! Father-Son Duo, Blue Eagle and Switch the Blue Eaglet, Defeat Archnemesis In Possible Final Battle*".

The photo was of him and Jack receiving the key to the city. Jack's smile was fake. And David....

David felt his jaw tighten, matching his expression in the photo.

He quickly replaced it with a practiced smile and gestured towards a comfortable chair in front of his desk.

"It sure does, but for now, let's talk insurance!"

It was a lazy Saturday afternoon, and Jack Dufraine was happy to have it. He looked around his room, gazing at his metal band and pro-wrestling posters as he took in this moment of tranquility. His father was working at the insurance office and he was done with his homework, which meant he had the house to himself. A chance to focus on the article he was reading, "Rehabilitation and Recidivism: How Support For Prisoners Leads to Less Crime", without interruption.

He couldn't focus. He couldn't absorb the material. His mind couldn't get itself off the events of the last week.

After the conversation in the car and the realization that Jasper had saved the city, he really thought his father had come around to his way of thinking on how to be a better superhero. On how to make a difference by doing more than punching out bad guys.

And maybe even came around on Jack's ability to be a superhero on his own one day.

Instead, his father had become even colder. More critical. And seemingly less confident in Jack's ability to even be a sidekick.

He placed his laptop off to the side and stared at the ceiling. What had happened? Why was his dad acting like this?

And was he right?

Was Jack just never going to be ready to be an independent superhero?

That's when he felt and heard the buzzing. He pulled his phone out of his black cargo pants and saw that a notification appeared. It was the police scanner app. His heart sank when he read the alert.

"NOTICE: SUPERVILLAIN WAVE RUNNER ATTACKING HERALD CITY TECH EXPO."

Wave Runner was one of their villains. He was part of the Blue Eagle Rogues Gallery. Which meant it was time to leap into action.

Jack shot to his feet. He ran a hand through his black hair, brushing a lock of it away from his eyebrow. His father would get annoyed if he didn't get it cut soon, or started styling it again so it was neater and more clean cut.

He thought back to the key to the city ceremony the other day. And his father's comment.

As much as he liked longer hair, he would get it cut short and neat. Perhaps that would get Blue Eagle off his back.

But that didn't matter right now. It was time for action.

He scrolled through his contacts. He found his father's number and his thumb hovered over the screen, ready to initiate the call.

His thumb hovered over the screen, ready to initiate the call.

He was ready to initiate the call.

"No," he whispered.

He didn't initiate the call.

He put the phone away, then lifted his shirt to reveal his costume underneath.

"I got this," he declared.

Epilogue

Night settled over Herald City. The half moon cast a light over the city, and the clouds projected a moving shadow over the skyline.

On the rooftop of one of the better maintained buildings in the rundown 5th Street Slums, Switch approached the rooftop entrance cabin, wearing a dark hoodie, T-shirt, and sweatpants.

He wasn't alone on the rooftop.

"It's been awhile," growled the figure standing in the shadows of the cabin.

"It has," said Switch.

There was a pause.

"The old man know about this?" asked the figure, his voice low and guttural. Switch couldn't remember him ever not sounding like he was growling.

"No," said the teen sidekick.

Another pause. "Trouble at home?" asked the figure, a hint of mockery in his voice.

"I want to be a superhero," declared Switch.

"I thought you already were a superhero."

"A real one. Not a sidekick."

"You want to leave the nest."

"Yes. But I can't," said Switch. His gaze lowered. "Blue Eagle is right. With my powers the way they are, I can't be a superhero on my own. But *you* can train me. Teach me how to fight without powers. To fight with weapons. To move without being seen. To be intimidating to criminals so they won't want to fight."

A contemplative moan came from under the figure's breath. To Switch, it sounded like a feral snarl.

"Lofty goals, kid," said the man. "Do you really know what you're getting into? If you want to be the kind

of superhero I am?" There was a pause
before—almost as a taunt—he added, "I *kill*."

Switch stiffened. "I don't."

"It should stay that way," the man quickly said. "You
don't have what it takes to be a superhero, but it ain't
because of your powers. It's because things aren't
always so whimsical and adventurous outside of the
Blue Eagle bubble, and you're too young and have
had it too good to make it in *my* world, where you
hit the streets and see things that will make you lose
sleep for years."

There was another pause as the figure let out a
defeated sigh. Even the sigh sounded like a vicious
snarl.

"But you're gonna be out there anyway, so it's better
you be prepared than not," he conceded. "I'll do it.
I'll train you."

"Good," said Switch, keeping his face and voice even.
"And remember the one thing I specifically asked of
you."

"I remember, and I'll abide by it," said the man.

He turned and stepped out of the shadows of the
cabin. In the moonlight, his heavily scarred face,

white streak of hair, and massive muscular frame were as visible as day. His black costume prominently displayed his impressive, intimidating physique, baring the left side of his chest entirely.

And even in the darkness of night, there was no escaping the stern, contemptuous gaze of the man.

"Just like you asked, I won't go easy on you," said Bloodpayne, "even if you are my brother."

Thank you for reading the prequel novel for my main series, *SWITCH and the Challengers Bravo!*

You've just stepped into a world with a vast array of heroes, villains, civilians, and other strange beings. One brimming with history....and secrets.

Before your very eyes, Switch just took his first step into a brave new world, one where he is a superhero on his own terms. And one where he is the leader of his own team of teenage heroes!

While you wait for Book 1, allow me to introduce you its main characters in

SWITCH and the Dossier

Get to know the Challengers Bravo–Switch, Moon Shadow, Animalady, and Bionic Boy–in this FREE short story, available exclusively to subscribers of the TienSwitch mailing list.

Subscribe to the newsletter and more at www.tienswitch.com!

And check me out on BlueSky and Facebook!

Don't miss my other series

The Adventures of BLUE EAGLE

Fun, lighthearted adventures of a superhero and his sidekick saving the day!

Blue Eagle is Herald City's superhero defender, and Switch the Blue Eaglet is his sidekick. Together, they go on numerous exciting, funny, suspenseful, and wacky adventures, beating the bad guys and saving the world!

Don't miss these exciting tales. Check out *The Adventures of BLUE EAGLE* today. Volume 1 is on sale now!

For more exciting superhero action, be sure to keep
up with all my other work in the BLUE EAGLE
UNIVERSE at tienswitch.com!

Acknowledgments

Thank you to Marcel and James for being in my writing corner the entire way since 2020. A double thanks to Marcel for reading every word I've written so far, published or unpublished, and everything I've written since the *Stony Brook Press* and FictionPress.

Thank you to my ARC readers, including Jack Qiu, Michele W, Kathryn Mc, kevinsbookcase, W. S. Dawkins, and all the rest of you.

Thank you to all my readers and followers on Royal Road. You were the first to experience the Blue Eagle Universe as far back as 2021 and my first fans of this endeavor.

And thank you to everyone on and offline that supported my writing endeavors and gave me advice on how to put words onto paper and get people to read them.

About the Author

Joseph Safdia, aka "TienSwitch", is possibly the greatest superhero fiction author of the 21st and/or 22nd Centuries, depending on time travel technology, aging, and sales.

He is a lifelong superhero fan from New York City, the centerpoint of Marvel superheroics, and picked up his first Spider-Man comic when he was 6. Now, he is creating an entire superhero mythology centered around Blue Eagle, Switch, and Herald City.

In his civilian identity, Joseph is an Anti-Money Laundering (AML) investigator, fighting real life villains who break the law and try to hide it or peddle superweapons to tyrannical rulers abroad.

You can find more of his work—including an incredible blog dedicated to superheroes—over at his website, www.tienswitch.com.

BEFORE YOU GO....

Customer reviews allow independent authors to continue sharing their stories. If you enjoyed this book, or if you hated this book (I hope not!), please leave a review on the platform you purchased it from.

It only takes a minute, but it means a lot to me.